# MEGACHURCH

# MEGACHURCH

### Worldwide Revival

## Robert A. Allen

RESOURCE *Publications* · Eugene, Oregon

MEGACHURCH
Worldwide Revival

Resource Publications
An Imprint of Wipf and Stock Publishers
199 W. 8th Ave., Suite 3
Eugene, OR 97401

www.wipfandstock.com

PAPERBACK ISBN: 978-1-6667-1484-5
HARDCOVER ISBN: 978-1-6667-1485-2
EBOOK ISBN: 978-1-6667-1486-9

JUNE 21, 2021

*To Carmen, my Song*

*whose heart sings like the uncaged bird,*

*created for the privileged purpose of praise.*

## Timothy 3 Plan

Above reproach

Husband of one wife

Temperate

Self-controlled

Respectable

Hospitable

Skillful in teaching

Not overindulging in wine

Not a bully

Gentle

Not contentious

Free from the love of money

*ST. PAUL'S LETTER TO TIMOTHY*


"The truth will make you free."

*ST. JOHN'S GOSPEL*


"Your word is truth."

*ST. JOHN'S GOSPEL*

# CONTENTS

# CHAPTER ONE

He had to find her. Somewhere in the amusement park, a kaleidoscope of frantic motion and color, Serenity Edwards had to be found. For her own sake. For her father's sake. For his sake.

No, not for his sake. That could never happen. Sere would never allow herself to be found for his sake. But she still had to be found.

Soft winds from the Kansas prairie relieved the oppressive heat of an unusual early October heat wave. The flashing lights of the newly-opened Spirit of the Spire Inspirational Theme Park welcomed him along with thousands of visitors from around the world who came to experience the Bible brought to life in the great tradition of Silver Dollar City, the Six Flags franchise, and Disney. Blinking marquees proclaimed the glories of the attractions:

> Walk on the Sea of Galilee with the Apostle Peter wearing transparent floating water shoes.

> Ride the Wilderness Sojourn out of Egypt through the Red Sea and experience the terrifying thunder and lightning of Mount Sinai.

> Soar high over the park in the Whirlwind of Elijah's Chariot.

> Plunge down the nearly vertical slope of the Fall of Man Roller Coaster.

> Experience the ninety-five turns and twists in ninety-five seconds on Luther's 95 Thesis, guaranteed to nail you to the Wittenberg Wall.

Visit the ultimate spook house appropriately named Satan's Sanctuary.

Step into the Multi-plex and thrill to the re-enactments of Creation, Passion and Apocalypse through Virtual Reality.

Enjoy a wedding at the Bride of the Lamb Chapel.

Ben Morris hurried through the food court, drenched with the diverse odors of cinnamon, bacon, cotton candy and roasted almonds, past Jordan's Crossing Café advertising John the Baptist Locust dipped in chocolate, St. Peter's Fish Sticks and Moses's Manna Wafers for the weight conscious.

Why wouldn't Serenity answer her phone? He knew the entire complex featured abundant wi-fi access—it was one of her priorities. So why didn't she use it herself? Nothing else escaped her detailed attention to minutiae—that was one of the things he loved about her.

No, he couldn't say that. It was one of the things he most admired about her. Not loved. Never loved. No use of the "L" word. He could applaud her creativity. He could admire her business acumen. He could marvel at her ability to multi-task. But he couldn't love her. He could never allow that. And yet he did.

The crowds thronging the entertainment venue conceived by the creative mind of Serenity Edwards rivaled in numbers those who personally attended her father's church each week. She would never match the total impact of InSpire Ministries because the Theme Park could not be transmitted via satellite to the homes of those who followed Dr. Ernst Edwards on their PCs, IPads, Smart Phones, and other devices every Sunday. Six days out of seven in any given week, however, those who paid to play in the Spirit of the Spire outnumbered the ones who found places in the 75,000 seats of InSpire on Sunday morning. They would never exceed the millions around the world who listened to Ernst Edwards remotely. Critics liked to say he made waves—he was content to say that he rode the wave. InSpire Ministries had resembled many other so-called megachurches across the nation until the advent of the Reversal of Babel app. The story had since entered the annals of religious history alongside the Gutenberg Bible and televangelism. A young inventor walked into his office seeking funding for a new phone app. Ernst immediately recognized the possibilities. The app listened to the language of any person who spoke into the phone and immediately translated all replies into that language. Instant effective communication. Starting with just six languages, the inventor added another one hundred seventy-four. With every app came a personal presentation of the gospel from Dr. Edwards, creating the wave of worldwide revival he had successfully ridden.

Ben paused at the entrance to the Bride of the Lamb Wedding Chapel where a young couple exchanged vows in front of a crowd of strangers. The Chapel had been one of Serenity's offbeat, but fortuitous, hunches. To think that people loved weddings so much they would attend that of a stranger had seemed ludicrous to him, a viewpoint he had not failed to share with her. Even more so had been the suggestion that people would book their weddings in such a venue. He had been wrong. The Chapel weddings calendar now accepted reservations a year in advance.

She wasn't there.

Ben thought he spotted her in front of the Gutenberg Bible Museum, one of his favorite exhibits. Slightly taller than the average woman with auburn black hair that captured the soft black tones and combined them with warm reds. An erect carriage which conveyed authority and energetic movement portraying her love of life. But when the woman in view turned to face him, she had none of the effervescence which shone from the eyes of Serenity and attracted the attention of everyone who saw her. He knew he was not alone in thinking her the most beautiful woman since Nefertiti. He had seen young boys walk into lampposts simply because they could not take their eyes off her.

The ever-present soundtrack providing the background music for the Spirit of the Spire experience switched to the melody known to a previous generation as "Knick Knack Paddy Whack" and to their children as the "Barney Theme Song." Visitors paid no attention, except for those who started singing "I love you, you love me" before being stared down by their companions. But the park attendants moved immediately into alert mode. Both entrance and exit gates closed, with ticket-takers and exit guards providing elaborate explanations as to why ingress and egress were suddenly halted. Employees checked their phones for a description of the missing child. Serenity's Amber alert system had never failed. Almost daily a child became separated from parents, but from the beginning she had sworn that no stranger-danger episodes would ever take place in her theme park.

Ben recognized the alert signal. Regretting the fact that he had never downloaded the Amber alert app, he walked up to the nearest ticket agent. "May I borrow your phone, please?"

"I beg your pardon?" The young lady started to hand him the phone and then jerked it back, suddenly realizing she didn't know him.

"Sorry. I should have identified myself." He handed her his InSpire ID. "Assistant to Dr. Ernst Edwards."

"Of course, Dr. Morris. I should have recognized you. Here." She handed the phone to him with a glazed look of idolization, as if she had just been approached by the President.

"Seven years old," he read. "Red blouse. White shorts. Blue shoes. No hat. Last seen carrying a Queen Esther scepter. Where would I find quadrant twenty-seven?" He handed back the phone.

"Just beyond the Billy Sunday Tabernacle. Two quadrants to your right."

She sighed quietly as he walked away. What a story she would have for her roommate tonight. Benjamin Morris himself. The most eligible bachelor in the entire ministry. She couldn't even remember what she had said to him. Had she really said, "I beg your pardon?" Those eyes. That smile. She wondered if he would remember seeing her if they met again. He looked even better than he did on her smart phone. She should have taken a picture. That's exactly what her roommate would say. "You should have taken a picture."

Ben spotted Serenity as soon as he rounded the corner of the Billy Sunday Tabernacle. She sat on a bench beside an obviously distraught mother, the calm center of an emotional tornado. Her face radiated the concern for the missing child.

"Tell me once again what happened just before you realized Erin was missing," he heard her ask the mother in quiet tones.

"The girls went into the bathroom together. I specifically told them to stay together," the mother glanced at a young girl crying on the other end of the bench.

"It's all my fault," said the girl, wiping her tears on her mother's scarf. "I thought she finished washing her hands. I told her to come. I thought she was right behind me. I didn't leave her on purpose."

"It's not your fault," said the mother. "You can't blame yourself. We don't blame you. We just want to find Erin. We will find her, won't we? Please tell me you'll find my little girl."

Serenity nodded and placed her hand over the trembling hand of the mother. "So, your daughter came out of the restroom without Erin? How long ago was that?"

"Just a few minutes ago. We told one of your park attendants as soon as we realized she was missing. Three minutes? Maybe five? I don't know."

"She can't leave the park. We have sent out an alert so that no one can enter or leave. She's still nearby. I promise you we will find her."

Ben knew exactly when Serenity spotted him. How many times had he warmed to that expression of friendship on her face and wished for more? He moved through the crowd to stand near the bench where they sat.

"Mrs. Taylor? This is Dr. Benjamin Morris, assistant to my father. I assure you that every resource at our disposal has been mobilized to find your daughter. Ben would you sit here and talk with Erin's mother for a time? I have an idea."

Serenity gave him no option, pulling him down to the bench while standing up and heading off in the direction of the restroom. Grabbing a park attendant on the way, she whispered something in the girl's ear which caused her to start running around the side of the building. Serenity walked into the restroom and disappeared from sight.

"Mrs. Taylor, is it?" said Ben. "Tell me about your daughter."

"Erin is only seven. This is her first visit to the Spirit of the Spire, and she was so excited to come. It's Evelyn's birthday." The woman nodded toward the little girl curled up next to her on the bench. "She's nine. We watch you and Dr. Edwards every Sunday even when we can't make it to the Spire for services. My husband and I love the way he leads us through the Bible verse by verse. You will find Erin, won't you?"

"I have no doubt about that. Serenity has equipped the theme park with the latest technology for that exact reason. She determined from the beginning that no child would ever be in danger while enjoying the Spirit of the Spire. Did you know that she planned the park and presided over its construction in every detail?"

"I heard it was her Freedom Project just like all those others Dr. Edwards approves. It's so wonderful the way he inspires creativity and helps fund the dreams of those who respond to his preaching."

Ben pursued the subject, knowing it would be the best way to keep her mind away from the worry about a missing child. "I remember the day she made her proposal. She had just graduated from the university, but the idea had been incubating since a childhood visit to Six Flags. Serenity placed a complete blueprint of the entire park on her father's desk along with a six-hundred-page proposal detailing the rationale and description of every ride, restaurant, attraction, and venue, supported by cost estimates and potential income revenues."

Evelyn spotted them first and jumped up with a squeal of excitement, racing toward the young girl who had just come around the corner of the restroom hand in hand with Serenity.

"Erin. Oh, Erin! You're back!" She hugged her sister around the neck and pulled her toward their mother.

Mrs. Taylor opened her arms, making way for both girls to be included in a motherly embrace. Ben stood to the side, providing room for Serenity to join them. He noticed that the theme music had already switched from Barney to "Kiss the Girl" from *The Little Mermaid.*

"Where have you been, dear? We were so worried."

Serenity answered on behalf of the crying child. "I remembered something like this happening before. There are two entrances to the restroom, one on either end of the building. It is so easy to get turned around and go out the wrong door. She was right there, looking up and down the next street over for the two of you."

"How can we ever thank you?" said Mrs. Taylor.

"No thanks are necessary. We rejoice with you in this happy outcome. In fact, I want you to be my guests for lunch. Have the girls been to the Table in the Presence of My Enemies?"

"Really?" Erin wiped away the tears. "Can we go there, Momma? That's where you can sling rocks at Goliath and watch him fall if you hit him in the forehead. Can we go, Momma? Please?"

"Would you like to join us Ben?" said Serenity.

"I would love to, but I'm afraid that Miss Edwards and I are going to have to entrust you Taylors to one of her talented park attendants." He motioned toward the girl who had earlier set off on a mission for Serenity. "Would that be all right, Mrs. Taylor? This young lady will make sure they treat you right at the Table as guests of the Spire."

"Of course, Dr. Morris. I know both of you are busy. The girls and I appreciate the invitation. As you can see, they can't wait to take on Goliath. Thank you so much Miss Edwards, for finding Erin."

Ben waited until Serenity gave each of the girls and their mother farewell hugs before turning to leave, fully expecting her to follow him. Instead, she tapped him on the shoulder, and he found himself face to face with arched eyebrows and blazing eyes.

"What exactly do you think you are doing?" The clenched teeth kept others from hearing the exchange while communicating her frustration far more effectively than a shout. "I needed to go with them. For the sake of public relations. You have no business issuing orders here in the park even if you are my father's assistant. You are the most irritating, arrogant . . . '

He had done it again, managing to provoke her when all he wanted to do was demonstrate his care and concern. Ben grabbed her hard and hurried her along the path toward the nearest exit. "We've been through all of that already. Goliath will be an adequate substitute. You're needed at the Spire. Your father is dying."

# CHAPTER TWO

D
r. Edwards's executive suite on the seventeenth floor of the Spire was not where Serenity had expected Ben to bring her. The trip from the theme park had been marked by silence as she fumed, and he rushed her along. The fact that her father was sitting behind his kidney-shaped oak desk looking remarkably spry provided a second surprise. The only indication that Ben may have been telling the truth came from the fact that he did not try to stand up when she came through the door. Her father had always been a perfect gentleman.

"Serenity, I am so thankful Ben has been able to find you. I'm not sure why I spend all that money on your phone bill each month when you won't even use it." He delivered the words with a smile that erased any scolding.

"If you really supported my phone habit it would be because you love me, Dad. I've been on my own plan since I turned eighteen. Now what is this nonsense about your being sick?" Serenity walked around behind the desk, kissed him on the cheek and crouched down beside his chair. "You don't have my permission to die, you know."

"Right. I haven't given permission either, but the doctors haven't asked for it. The cancer has returned and this time they're saying four to eight weeks. The biopsy report arrived this morning, and I sent Ben out on search-and-rescue."

She gripped his hand and tried to smile. That was her father, straightforward as always. He had never sugar-coated anything for her ever since the day they had brought her mother back from the hospital and set up round-the-clock nursing care for her dementia.

"So, what are you doing here at the office? You should be home in bed."

"That's probably what John's daughter said when he took that trip to the Isle of Patmos. But just think what we would have lost if he had taken her advice."

"I give up. Not that you have ever listened to my advice anyway. Have you and Ben decided to add another chapter to the Bible? I thought Revelation warned against that practice. He made it sound like the Apocalypse had already arrived."

Ernst reached for the glass of water on his desk and swallowed with obvious difficulty. Serenity looked up to see Ben standing beside her with one of the chairs from the boardroom table on the other side of the room. She smiled her thanks in spite of her frustration and sat down next to her father's office chair. Ben took a seat on the other side of the desk and Serenity finally noticed that another person had joined them, her father's lawyer, Lawrence Wiley.

"I do plan to take your advice," her father said, setting down the glass. "No apocalypse. No new revelation. But the doctors have warned me that my time will be no more. Occasion demands that my Timothy Three Plan go into action."

Serenity grinned. A Timothy Three Plan. Definitely her father's touch. He had named her first car Jehu's Chariot when a patrolman had ticketed her for speeding the same week she got her license. One of her high school boyfriends, a young man of whom he had distinctly disapproved, had been given the nickname of Shallum by her father, even though the boy's name was Hal. Hal had never figured it out, but she had. King Shallum had reigned in Israel only one month, and her dad, in his own inimitable way, was suggesting that her relationship with Hal be as short as the king's tenure. It was.

The lawyer laid a file of papers on the desk. "This plan for succession dates back to the original incorporation documents for the Spire which our firm filed. Your father had come to admire the business acumen of a preacher from Los Angeles by the name of McPherson—Aimee Semple McPherson. She had learned from observation the problems which could arise from church members who took issue with the way a congregation was administered. McPherson incorporated her entire ministry with power invested in a three-person board—Aimee, her mother and her personal secretary. The stability of that arrangement enabled them to flourish in spite of the upheaval of the depression years, vicious criticism by fellow preachers, and even government persecution in the person of the Los Angeles district attorney. That is why, ever since day one of InSpire Ministries, all official business has been handled by three people, Dr. Edwards, your mother, and you."

"She knows all that, and what she doesn't know you can fill her in on later." Ernst picked up the file and opened it on the desk. "The details of the Timothy Three Plan, or simply T-3. I have assembled files on the men I find acceptable as my potential successors. Your task will be to visit with each one of them in person and make the final choice. If I am still alive at that time, I will approve the decision. If not, you will introduce him to the ministry at large. You are the only one who can do that legally, according to the documents Lawrence just referenced. But beyond that, you are the only one I would ever trust with the future of InSpire Ministries."

Serenity stood and wrapped her arms around her father. "Dad, it's me. You're not on camera now. I know how little you care for emotional scenes, but I'm going to cry right now and there's nothing you can do about it. You can call me a drama queen like you did when I was eleven, but that's not going to stop me."

As Ernst joined his daughter in a long overdue release of emotion, Ben and Lawrence quietly left them to their mutual grief.

For the next half hour, amid several episodes of tears, his vision for T-3 came to light. He wanted the ministry to thrive after his death, not stagnate. The legal technicalities had been entrusted to the lawyers, but he needed to share his heart with her. Serenity knew that the intimate, interpersonal communication they shared paralleled exactly the experience of people around the globe who listened to her father speak. No bombast. No inflated rhetoric. No flights of fancy. Just a loving, conversational discussion of the truth of God. The milk and meat of the word of God produced spiritual strength enabling holy living. Following him as he followed God. Description of his vision for T-3 fit the pattern of his entire ministry—exposition of biblical truth.

"Paul and Timothy. Father and son in the faith. Family connections permeate Paul's list of instructions for pastoral succession in the third chapter of his first letter to Timothy. God has not given your mother and I a son, but the next man who pastors InSpire Church will be my son in the faith just as Timothy was to Paul. He will be a role model of godliness. Not sinless, but forgiven. Not perfect, but growing more like Christ, the Perfect One, each day. A man chosen by God to lead His people must be calm and spiritually temperate, serious about the ministry, while at the same time finding joy in the strength of the Lord. He will bring order out of the chaos of administrative duties without elevating a sense of his own self-importance. The door to his office will always be open. He may not choose to follow my pattern of delivery, but the messages he shares will arise from diligent study of the Word. Addictions will not control him, even those theological addictions people refer to as hobby horses. Neither will he be controlled by temper tantrums or greed. Gentle, loving, gracious, and flexible will be characteristics by which people identify him as opposed to pugnacious, revengeful, and domineering. Each man on the list you have been given has been active in ministry for years. My successor will not be a novice."

How many times had she sat in services at the Spire and marveled at the rapt attention given to her father as he spoke. His ability to communicate directly to the hearts of those who listened had endeared him to an entire generation of faithful disciples. Whether they sat in the seats of the Spire, occupied the pews of the one hundred thirty-seven satellite churches, or tuned in from their own living rooms via live-stream, his calm confidence assured them of the fact that what they were learning came directly from the mind of God. How many times had she heard him explain how Bible study must move from understanding to interpretation, from interpretation to application, and from application to creative action. "Devotional reading becomes transformational as the Holy Spirit leads the believer into creative avenues of service for God based on the principles of the Word of God," he would often say. Her own development of the Spirit of the Spire Theme Park had been a direct result of that encouragement. Hundreds of other Freedom Projects had been energized and funded by InSpire Ministries. And now her father trusted her to determine its future direction.

Reaching out for the file which would reveal the names of possible successors and flesh out the responsibility with which she had been entrusted, Serenity realized that the desktop lay empty except for her father's open Bible. Lawrence must have picked up the folders when he and Ben left the room.

Her father held out an arm and allowed her to help him stand. "All the necessary legal arrangements have been made. You will find them in the documents. Lawrence will meet with you to go over the details. Ben has agreed to accompany you on the journey and handle the travel plans. I have just one more request before you leave. For the sake of legality, and love, would you go with me to tell your mother?"

Serenity nodded, brushing a final tear from her cheek. They needed to tell her mother.

# CHAPTER THREE

The penthouse home of Leila Edwards featured magnificent glass windows overlooking the Missouri River against the Kansas City skyline. Industrial-inspired sofas defined by heavy metals and textured materials contrasted with Scandinavian decorative pillows and area rugs. Stark and perfectly groomed, it presented the modern appearance of an old-fashioned parlor reserved for special occasions which had never arrived. The only contrast came from the nurse's station in front of a cabinet crowded with hospital equipment.

Leila's suite, just off the sterile entrance room, displayed a vision of childhood dreams fulfilled. Oversized figures of Cinderella, Sleeping Beauty, Rapunzel, and Ariel decorated the walls. Little Miss Muffet fled from the spider, and Tiger Lily ran away from Captain Hook. Her bed resembled a large shoe with the Old Woman and her children painted on the headboard and sides. Porcelain dolls dressed in exquisite costumes crowded shelves and peered out from drawers and toyboxes, all of which stood open. A plush Persian carpet featuring a chessboard design held life-size figures from Alice in Wonderland which tumbled in glorious disarray across the squares. A calico cat perched sleepily on one of the rooks.

At a small table in the center of the room, Serenity and her father saw the White Queen figurine taking tea with a petite figure dressed in a red and white pinafore.

"She's Alice today," the nurse whispered to Serenity as her father approached the table and took a seat beside his wife. "She has experienced one of her better days, but I need to warn you. She has not done well since your father grew ill. We haven't shared his diagnosis with her, but I think

13

she senses something. Her doctor compares it to Reflex Sympathetic Dystrophy Syndrome, where a person suffers from pain even after a wound is healed. But in this case, she seems to be suffering from Dr. Edwards's pain. There must be a very close emotional connection between them."

Serenity nodded. She had never witnessed any more loving emotional connection between two people than that of her parents, even though her mother had lived in a fantasy world for years. She took her place at the table and accepted an empty cup and saucer from the nurse. "Good afternoon, Mother."

The pinafore rustled stiffly as the frail figure reached a dainty hand across to the White Queen with a cup of sugar water she had just poured from a porcelain teapot. "Be careful now Queenie. Mustn't spill like you did yesterday. The Red Queen will have your head, you know."

"May we join your tea party, Mother?"

The eyes focused on her for just an instant, bright, cheerful and empty. Leila offered no indication of recognition, no encouraging sign that this once brilliant woman would ever return from her fantasy world.

"I trust the tea will suit your fancy m'lady. I borrowed the recipe from the Mad Hatter, if you must know." What began as the giggle of a little girl changed into a painful gasp, convulsing her entire body in bursts of shaking while her mouth remained frozen in an adolescent grin. Dr. Edwards gathered her into his arms, leaned her head against his shoulder, and patted her like an infant until the seizures subsided.

"That's the first one today," said the nurse. "The first one. Some days are better than others."

The marriage of Leila Ford and Ernst Edwards had been the talk of the town. America's sweetheart and Kansas City's pride and joy. The first wedding in the sparkling new Spire which was already making Kansas City the epicenter of evangelicalism. The birth of Serenity two years later had ended the bliss but not the marriage. Vows had been spoken. Promises had been made, and promises were meant to endure. For better or worse represented an entrance door to a life which swung both ways. For Ernst the better had become worse, but Leila enjoyed the best of medical care and the faithful love of a husband who demonstrated that love every day. As Serenity watched her father fold his arms around a wife who would never consciously return that embrace, she longed for one who would commit himself to her as unconditionally. She just wasn't sure there was anyone else in all the world like her father.

"I'm going away for a few days," she explained when the shaking had subsided and they were once again back at the tea party. "It won't be for long. I'll miss you, mother."

The cat, attracted by the clink of the cups and saucers, stretched lazily and wandered over to rub against Serenity's leg.

"Perhaps the Cheshire cat would like to join us," said Leila. Taking the teapot from the table, she placed a saucer on the floor and poured it full for the cat. "Is Prince Charming coming today?"

Serenity smiled, certain that her mother had already forgotten the embrace of her prince, but Ernst shook his head sadly. "That's not what she calls me. I have no idea who she thinks of as the prince. Her name for me is Humpty Dumpty."

"Humpty Dumpty? Really?" She grinned as she looked at the trim figure of her father, who she was certain had never lugged around an unnecessary pound.

"When she was pregnant, she teased me about my expanding waistline. Said that it matched hers and came up with that nickname. It seems to be the only memory she has of our lives together."

This time it was the daughter who sought comfort in the arms of her father while Leila focused her attention on the cat.

"Apparently not even that memory is enough to bring her back today. Perhaps she will respond to you." He handed her the forms from the lawyer, and she placed them on the table in front of her mother.

"Father needs you to sign something before I leave on my trip. Would you do that mother?" She spread out the legal papers authorizing succession, handing her mother a pen. With Ernst's help they showed her where to sign. A scribble and a giggle which didn't result in spasms accomplished their mission before Alice turned back to entertaining the White Queen and the Cheshire cat. She didn't even notice when they took their leave.

Dinner at The Capital Grille with Lawrence Wiley had not been on her agenda for the evening. A text message on her phone provided the invitation and details. Not the most romantic gesture, but she certainly wasn't looking for romance from the corporation lawyer. Just the facts, ma'am, just the facts, said her inner Joe Friday. Seared salmon with avocado and straight talk from her father's lawyer. That's all she wanted. The attorney seemed determined to avoid the legal straight talk until after the meal, however.

"It must have been a shock to hear the biopsy report. Your father has always seemed so strong. The man who could conquer every foe."

"Surprise? Yes and no. I've been aware of the cancer for some time. The rapid progress I find distressing." More distressing had been his choice to share the medical diagnosis in front of Ben and the lawyer, something she was not about to admit to Wiley. The entire meeting had been so unusual, so out of the ordinary for her father. Health had always been a private family matter, due perhaps to Leila's condition, which neither of them had been inclined to expose for public consumption. It bothered her that she had first heard about the report from Ben, even though it was her own fault for turning off her cellphone. Sometimes she imagined him trying to force himself into a position of becoming the son her father had always wanted. He didn't know his own father, so that would make sense. But she also knew the mental accusation wasn't fair. The T-3 Project proved her wrong. Her father trusted her even more than he did Ben.

Menus occupied their attention for a time as the waiter arrived to take their orders. The salmon for Serenity and a Prime Rib sandwich for Lawrence.

"Doctors have been known to get it wrong."

"Not this time. The biopsy simply confirmed what previous tests had already revealed. If my reaction seemed cold this afternoon, it's simply because I have already had adequate time to absorb the inevitable." She wasn't sure why she even needed to try to explain her emotions to the lawyer. Her best friend Beth had been with her to witness the tears, the personal recriminations for not insisting on regular medical checkups, the unanswered questions for God, and the anxiety over future care for her mother. Those were not topics suitable for dinner conversation with anyone else, especially a lawyer. In spite of frustration with his determination to postpone discussion of the legal ramifications of T-3, she forced herself to enjoy the meal.

"How long have you been with the firm now?" If he wanted small talk maybe she could get him to focus on himself. It worked with most people she knew. She had always been a good listener.

"Three years. Still working toward a partnership. Burnley, Wiley, and Associates. Not Wiley and Son. Father has been representing the Spire since day one. I believe you also worked with one of our partners when setting up the Theme Park."

"Burnley. He did excellent work. So, your father must have had a hand in writing the original incorporation papers."

"That's what he tells me. Your father walked into his office fresh out of seminary and announced a plan to revolutionize the church. 'God planned a universal church and that's what He deserves.' Those were the words my father still remembers from that first conversation. He wanted a plan of organization which would prevent any potential insurgence among staff—something he had seen in existing church structures. The triumvirate used by Aimee Semple McPherson provided their template."

"Father, mother, and me. I couldn't have been much more than a gleam in his eye at that time."

"That didn't matter. 'The third administrator of the corporation shall be the first-born child of the union between Ernst Edwards and Leila Ford Edwards' was the way he insisted the documents read. He determined that not even a family squabble would disrupt his plan, should more children join the family. 'If one of the administrators dies, the other two entities possess the sole legal empowerment for replacement.' Hence the Timothy Three Plan. A successor chosen by the board."

Serenity found it possible to enjoy the perfectly seasoned salmon placed in front of her by the waiter in spite of the tension of the day's events. Concentrating on their meals hindered further discussion until Lawrence washed down the final morsel of prime rib with mango-infused iced tea and shoved the tableware aside to make room for his files.

"I have worked closely with your father to prepare curriculum vitae concerning each of the prospects for succession to the Spire pulpit. I believe you will find everything you need to prepare yourself for the personal interviews. Your father prefers to have you visit each of them in their own backyard, as it were, rather than bringing them here, and rightly so. Seeing them in their own environment will provide insight beyond what might be expected from a sterile in-house dialogue. He expects the visible results of their endeavors to provide the most potent evidence."

Lawrence extracted three slim folders from his file and slid them across the table.

"Billy Wilson, Chicago, Illinois."

"Michal DeLoran, Denver, Colorado."

"Daniel Ellicott, Kandahar, Afghanistan."

Serenity opened the cover of the third folder. A glossy portrait of a young man, fully bearded and swathed in a black and white kaffiyeh which hung down over the shoulders of a brown robe stared back at her, the beard and mustache well-trimmed, framing a strong chin. A Nordic nose and brilliant blue eyes stood at variance with his sun-darkened skin and middle eastern garb.

"Ellicott. Of course. He looks so young. A recent picture?"

"Youth remains a factor in each of your father's choices. King David served his own generation. Your father served his own age as well. He believes it will require the initiative of one of their own to reach young hearts in a rapidly changing world. The global average median age stands at 29.6 percent."

She began to leaf through the folder as the lawyer continued.

"You will have adequate time on your flight to review the information, but allow me to provide a brief summary. Daniel graduated from the University of Minnesota with a degree in agriculture. Friendship with an Afghan student opened his eyes to the unique environmental challenges facing farmers in a country with only 58 percent arable land. Two-thirds of the country is covered by rugged mountains, beautiful but unsuitable for most crops. Opium has long been a top agricultural product along with fruit, nuts, wool, and wheat. Life expectancy is only forty-two. After accepting a position as advisor to the Kabul government, Daniel became aware of the spiritual needs as well. His efforts initially focused on the refugee camps, those displaced by the incessant wars which plagued the country. The story of the Afghan revival which spread through those camps has taken its place in church history alongside the Welsh revival and the Great Awakening. Recently, with the withdrawal of foreign troops, those new Christians have returned to their cities and villages controlled for centuries by mullahs. And yet his work has prospered. Conservative estimates suggest that nearly a million Afghans participate in the house church network organized by Daniel Ellicott."

Gazing again at the portrait, Serenity could almost see the passion and zeal which animated the mind of a man who dedicated himself to a people forgotten by the rest of the world. There were so many questions she needed to ask her father. Why these three? What if all of them refused? Why not one of the pastors from the satellite churches? She voiced one of them before even realizing she had translated her thoughts into words.

"Why? Why would father think he would fit here in Kansas City?"

The lawyer gathered up the stack of materials from the table, slid them back into the file folder, and handed the three dossiers to her while signing the check for the meal. His answer sounded sincere, if somewhat rehearsed, as if he had asked the question previously of himself.

"The Spire is no longer simply a product of Kansas City, Miss Edwards. It belongs to the world. Everyone owns a cell phone, even in a land of extreme poverty. Your father's messages are heard in Pashto and Dari. Ellicott has become fluent in those languages as well as Arabic. His house churches exist without pastoral leadership apart from his visits. They depend on technology, and this ministry provides the bread of life which feeds the hungry spirits of those Daniel reaches with the gospel. That's why your father wants you to visit him. To see for yourself how InSpire Ministries has impacted and coordinated with the Afghan revival. The urgency of your task demands immediate attention in light of your father's condition. The matter of succession must be determined before his demise. He insisted on prompt action during my last visit with him. You will find your tickets there in the folder. The Spire Gulfstream departs at 6:23 tomorrow morning."

# CHAPTER FOUR

Beth Guilford greeted Serenity at the door of the apartment they had shared until her recent wedding to Tony Guilford. Handing her a cup of Chai tea, she pointed her in the direction of an easy chair.

"You look terrible, Sere. Sit down before you collapse. Ben called. He said you might need some help packing. You've had quite a day."

"To say the least. What outfits might be suitable for a journey to Kandahar?" Serenity blew across the hot tea.

Beth tapped on her phone. "Let's see. Average high for September in Kabul would be twenty-eight degrees for a high and eleven for a low. Both Celsius."

"You expect me to multiply by one-point-eight and add thirty-two after the day I've had?"

"Eighty-two and fifty-one," said Beth. "It helps to be married to an accountant. So, temperate days and cool nights. Unless Kandahar is in the mountains. So, tell me—I assume Kandahar means Daniel Ellicott. Who else has your father included on his short list for this T-3 Plan?"

Sipping cautiously in order to avoid burning her tongue, Serenity pulled the photograph of Ellicott out of the file and handed it to her best friend. "Musician Michal DeLoran and football star Billy Wilson."

Beth rustled through the other files to extract similar glossies. "Definitely targeting the youth market. Not only young, but single if I remember correctly. Are you certain this is not a plan to marry off his beautiful and oh-so-eligible daughter?"

Her jerk on the handle of the cup produced the very scorched tongue she had been trying to avoid. "Really, Beth? Why is it that every newlywed thinks marital bliss provides the path to happiness for all her friends? Father wouldn't do that to me."

"Wouldn't? Or couldn't? I seem to remember something about the 'husband of one wife' in that Timothy three passage. Knowing your father, he wouldn't force you in that direction, but couldn't he be hoping God might do that work for him?"

Serenity smiled with pleasure at Beth's gentle teasing, remembering the many similar conversations before Beth had fallen hard for Tony. Their friendship, forged in a determination to resist confusing the will of God with the expectations of humanity, had grown stronger as Beth discovered love. It didn't surprise her at all that her friend desired the same for her.

"Father wants a successor, not a son-in-law."

"If you say so." She replaced the photographs. "Ellicott looks like a real wild man. And what about your date with Wiley Coyote tonight?"

"You must have heard that from Ben as well. Lawrence is an attorney with Burnley, Wiley, and Associates, Beth. Almost a partner. You can't hold a junior high foot race against him after all these years."

"Foot race nothing. It was field day. He cut the corner down in the woods or he never would have beat the Road Runner. He'll always be Wiley Coyote to me. Tony thinks so too."

"Tony thinks whatever you want him to think. He would take your side if the odds were a hundred to one." She drank the last of the tea and set the cup and saucer down on the coffee table. "So, what have you convinced him to think? It was a business lunch, not a date."

"Only that Wiley can be trusted as far as the day is long." Beth grabbed the teacup and carried it into the kitchen, calling the end of the comment over her shoulder. "As long as the day comes in December in Utqiagvik, Alaska.

"Well, anyway, it wasn't a date. We met for a meal. He apprised me of the plans for T-3 and that was it. At my father's request by the way."

"The lady doth protest too much, methinks. Who paid for the meal?"

"Thank you, Queen Gertrude. Just remember, if your frivolous conjecture about father's intentions prove true, Lawrence Wiley did not even make the short list. And I'm sure he billed the ministry for whatever I ate."

"But Daniel Ellicott made the list. I remember him from his Freedom Project presentation at the Spire. Very impressive. Military troops led by empire builders have invaded Afghanistan for years without success. He walks alone into an historical stronghold of Islam with nothing more than a Bible and a message of hope and emerges a spiritual conqueror."

"Succinct and true. But perhaps nothing more than being in the right place at the right time. Foreign troop withdrawals left a military vacuum. The failure of American administrations at nation building created unfulfilled promises of universal education. An economy in shambles and exposure to world cultures left a society baffled, disappointed, and ripe for change. Those could also explain the Ellicott success story."

Beth picked up the Ellicott photograph. "Strong chin. Norwegian nose. Passionate eyes. You could do worse, Sere."

"Put it away. I have luggage to pack, and you promised to help. The Timothy plan is not the Bachelorette meets the Fab Three, so get to work. I have a plane to catch."

The ministry Gulfstream G280 with a silver replica of the Spire on its tail graced the runway at Lee's Summit Municipal Airport ready for departure to Ahmad Shah Baba International Airport in Kandahar. The flight of more than 7,300 miles would require one stop in Italy for refueling. Ben found the pilot and copilot completing their final preflight checklist.

"Sure glad that you two know what you're doing. I've never understood how a 24,000- pound hunk of metal can leave the ground as gracefully as an eight-pound Canada Goose. How are Maxine and the little ones, Mel?"

The pilot shook his hand and pulled out his wallet to reveal photographs of twin boys, identical except for contrasting caps, one with the Royals insignia and the other for Sporting Kansas City. "The hats are the only way we can tell them apart, but I think they're catching on and switching them if one of them thinks he's in trouble."

"Still wrestling in total silence when you send them to their room to work out their disagreements? Getting cuter every day." Ben returned the photos and rescued his suitcase from the copilot who had started up the stairs with his luggage. "You don't need to carry that Ashley. Rumor has it that you and Jerome are planning to jump into the parental pool before long. Better reserve your strength for the possibility of rambunctious twins like Melvin's here."

"You're as bad as Jerome, always telling me to put my feet up. I'm only eight months along and the morning sickness has long since passed."

"Too much information." Ben covered his ear with the hand which wasn't busy with his bag. "But congratulations. I expect you'll be flying right up until your due date."

"If my hubby will let me. But Uncle Melvin here says he won't help with the delivery after being there when the twins were born, so I might need to limit my travel to short hops. Fourteen hours to Afghanistan leaves me a long way away from my doctor."

Ben had just arrived at the top of the moveable stairs when a sporty red Mazda pulled up next to the plane. Beth Guilford hopped out of the driver's seat and headed back to pop the trunk, but his eyes focused on the passenger. Did she even realize how beautiful she was? Hair that reflected the rays of the early morning sun, providing a halo effect around her face. The intelligent sparkle in her eyes which challenged the observer to think deeply before engaging her in debate. A confident stride warning of a no-nonsense approach to life. Cleopatra and Guinevere combined couldn't begin to compare to Serenity Edwards. Was he the only one who saw it?

"Let me take those Beth," he called. "I really appreciate your Uber-replacement service this morning." He set down his own bag, raced down the steps and lifted two heavy cases out of the trunk, rolling them toward the plane. "Tony tells me congratulations are in order."

"Beth!" Serenity grabbed her friend by both hands and danced across the tarmac. "When were you going to tell me? When are you due? Have you had an ultrasound yet? Boy or girl? I can't believe you didn't tell me."

Beth smiled. "Apparently Tony couldn't keep his mouth shut. We just confirmed it with the doctor this week. I'm barely three months along. We haven't even told our parents yet."

"I'm going to be an aunt. Not really. But I'll feel like one. You'll name her after me of course."

"Since you already have a name, I guess they'll have to." Ben stopped to observe the quiet satisfaction on the face of Beth and the flurry of emotions animating Sere. Surely others must see the appeal of her effervescence.

"Have to what?"

"Have to name her after you. They can't name her before you."

"Typical male." She turned back toward Beth, dismissing him through her actions. "This is so exciting. I can't wait. You'll send me pictures of the ultrasound, right?"

"Why don't you just wait for the birth?" Ben called loudly from the door of the plane. "Then we can make this trip six months from now. Melvin and Ashley won't mind. She could even stay around for her own appointment with parturition."

"You can use the word childbirth," she yelled up the stairs. "Even pregnancy. They are not dirty words." Sere gave Beth a big hug. "Gotta go. Morris the Thesaurus, Mr. 'Why Use A Simple Word when Embellishment Beckons' grows anxious. Tell Tony I'm proud of him even if he did spill the beans to Ben first."

The interior of the Gulfstream had been renovated to accommodate a desk and credenza for Dr. Ernst, making it look more like a pastor's study than an airplane cabin. Comfortable sofas lined the walls. Overstuffed recliners grouped around a round table provided space for conferencing or meals. Once they had attained cruising altitude, Ashley came back from the cockpit to offer them breakfast.

"This plane practically flies itself," she said as she set out juice glasses, muffins, and a plate of waffles. "Melvin only needs me when he takes breaks, so consider me your flight attendant as well as the co-pilot. The galley has just about anything you might want except for fresh salmon. We only provide that during stop-overs in Alaska."

"That means you can join us for breakfast." Ben stood to help with the place settings and directed Ashley toward one of the overstuffed chairs. "You probably skipped it leaving as early as we did from KC."

"Thanks, Ben. Phil insisted on hitting the drive-through at McDonald's, so I did have a bacon, egg, and cheese sandwich, but I'd never turn down one of the muffins Dr. Ernst insists on stocking for these flights."

Serenity accepted the plates Ben handed to her. "I don't think Dad has ever started a day without a Blueberry muffin. I grew up thinking muffins were the third ordinance. How long have you been working for the ministry, Ashley?"

"Two years this summer. Melvin brought me over with him from Midwest Air. We had worked together there ever since I finished flight school."

"Melvin's her uncle," added Ben. "You know how much your father likes to hire within the family. I'm probably the only person working in the Spire who isn't related to some other employee. How many seconds should I heat these in the microwave, Ashley?"

"No more than thirty. The catering service delivered them this morning. They were probably still warm when they stocked the galley."

"Is Mike still driving for them?"

"Sure is. Just as prompt as usual."

Serenity poured syrup on her waffle and took a tentative bite. She had never been a breakfast person, but warm waffles at 30,000 feet, early in the morning, looked appealing. "Is there anyone you don't know, Ben? You're just like my father. I swear he could walk through the secretarial pool at the Spire, call every employee by name, and remember the ages of their children and the make of their car."

"I don't pay much attention to what people drive," said Ben. "But you flatter me by comparing me to your father. I've seen him meet a waitress at a restaurant and know her mother's maiden name, what classes she enrolled in that semester, and when her grandparents emigrated from Botswana even before the meal we ordered had arrived."

"That's my Dad. I used to admire his ability—until he turned his detective talents to questioning my boyfriends. One of them told me he could feel the bright light of the interrogation room turn on every time he walked through the front door."

Ben set the warm muffins on the table. "Is that what he's expecting from you in these interviews? No harsh lighting, of course, but enough information to make a decision concerning the direction of the ministry?"

"Apparently. But you probably know more about that than I do. His lawyer left me with a trainload of unanswered questions which I expect you and Dad have discussed in detail."

"Such as?"

"Why these three? Each has a successful ministry and a large following, but the contrasts with father's approach couldn't be greater."

"Would you like me to leave?" Ashley wrapped up her muffin in a napkin. "I should probably check on Melvin anyway."

"No. You have the itinerary. Kandahar, Denver and Chicago. Ellicott, DeLoran, and Wilson. We're all in this together. You're welcome to stay. So, what do you think, Ben? Surely you and father have discussed this."

Ben took a large bite out of the muffin, trying to give himself time to plan out a response. She had listed only three, not four. Apparently, Lawrence had shirked part of his responsibility for some unknown reason. Should he be grateful or ticked off? The fact that Serenity had not been given the fourth file would make it easier for him to participate in the trip as an impartial observer. She would consider him a colleague rather than a prospect. He would be free to advise without the advice back-firing and degenerating into the fruitless arguments which seemed to characterize their frequent interactions. On the other hand, knowing that she would at some point discover the truth made it very likely that she would be infuriated with him for not revealing the total plan up front. He decided to take that risk and use the oversight to his advantage, at least on the trip to Afghanistan.

"When your father first conceived this particular approach to succession, he made himself face the inevitable question of future effectiveness. His generation responded to the service style of the Spire beyond what anyone would have predicted. Who would have thought that religious worship without music would appeal to thousands of listeners?"

"I always wondered about that," said Ashley. "The first time I stepped into the Spire and didn't see any instruments, or choir loft, or worship leader, I thought I must be in the wrong building. Not even a piano."

"People questioned that decision more than any other choice he made," said Serenity. "He explained it to me in terms of rival constituencies. Musical styles had become the most divisive issue in the American church, not to mention the rest of the world. Churches split right down the middle with half of the members coming to a traditional service and the other half attending contemporary worship. Those who listened to Southern Gospel believed it to be the style used in heaven, while those who embraced Rap and Rock remained convinced it offered the only means of reaching youth with the Gospel. Rather than enter the fray, father eliminated the problem. People could listen to whatever they desired outside the Spire, but within those walls they would listen only to the spoken Word."

"And it worked," said Ben. "Sixty minutes of expository preaching broken up only by Freedom Project reports."

"That was another shock." Ashley started clearing off the table. "No offering. Every other megachurch leader seemed to spend more time raising money than sharing the message. Here were people talking about how the Spire had invested in them and how thankful they were to share the blessing with the one who had encouraged their creativity."

"My first day at the Spire happened to coincide with the testimony from the Deuchmans," said Ben. "They had visited the Spire and noticed immediately the use of holograms which projected the image of your father directly in front of every person in the auditorium. It amazed them to realize he could sit in a chair and hold a personal conversation with 75,000 people at once. When the background scene around him changed to the banks of the Jordan River or the desert of Mount Sinai, it blew their minds. They took that idea and applied it to road signs. Instead of a stop sign or signal light, cities could place signs right in the middle of intersections where no one could miss them. Since they were virtual, cars could drive right through them. When departments of transportation began to use their innovations, accidents plunged and Deuchmans experienced surging profits. When advertisers caught on and purchased the product, earnings went through the ceiling. On that day the family contributed over seven million dollars to the Spire as a blessing offering for the initial investment from the ministry."

"Which brings me right back to my question. What would any of these three add to what the ministry is already doing? He already took Frost's path less traveled, and that has made all the difference. Why go back to the road not taken?"

Ben shrugged. "I guess that's what your father wants you to discover. With his overall emphasis on Christian creativity, he wants to explore every possible option. He's seen too many organizations simply wither up and die when its founder moves off the scene. The old adage 'Everything rises and falls on leadership' works great when you are rising, but it's not of much use during a fall."

"Speaking of leadership, Melvin must be wondering what happened to me. Thanks for your help with breakfast. Prime Rib's on the menu for supper. Actually, with the time zones we pass through, you can call the meals by any name you desire. Let me know if you need anything before then." Ashley lifted herself out of the comfortable chair and headed back toward the cockpit.

Ben wasn't sure he wanted Ashley to leave. He had worked with Serenity in the past, but most often within a group setting. The first four years he was with the ministry she had been away at college. During the last two years the planning and construction of the theme park had monopolized most of her time. Not that being alone with her was something he dreaded—just the opposite. He longed for her company, delighted in the conversations they had shared, able to recall them almost word for word. What he feared was the possibility that she would find him pedantic or boring, nerdy even. Sometimes it seemed as if years of homeschooling and pursuit of a seminary degree had qualified him for everything except interpersonal relationships. Not once in Advanced Hebrew class had they ever discussed making small talk with someone you adored. He stood as Ashley excused herself, carried the breakfast plates and utensils into the small galley, and turned to find that Serenity had moved to one of the sofas which lined the walls of the plane. He took a seat on the opposite wall.

"Was there another question Attorney Wiley failed to answer?"

"Do you want the entire list? What will happen to the ministry if they all refuse? Why hasn't father considered one of the pastors from the satellite churches? Why didn't he just have each of these men fly into KC for an interview? They've all been there before to give Freedom Project testimonies. He could just as well have done this himself before he fell sick. Why leave it all up to me?"

The one question he wanted to answer, "Why me?" remained out of bounds. Answering that question would be like unleashing the floodgates of Hoover Dam, wiping out everything below. It could not be answered without revealing his personal esteem for her business acumen, his respect for her quick wit, his praise for her wisdom. No one possessed a greater passion for the ministry, stronger insight into what the future might hold, or a more genuine, heart-felt desire for its continued success than Serenity Edwards. He totally agreed with the decision Ernst had made when designing T-3. Even though he knew that Dr. Edwards's evaluation of his daughter was predisposed toward admiration due to their familial relationship, he agreed completely with the conclusion. The path forward deserved to be explored under her leadership as a trail guide. He longed to reveal the multiple conversations with her father leading up to that decision, something simply impossible for him to voice without revealing his own heart. He dared not block the future path he desired, but feared to walk. Instead, he chose the easier question.

"We talked about bringing each one to KC, but rejected that idea because of the value of seeing each man in his own environment. A carpenter providing formal project blueprints in your office presents a totally different image from seeing him on the job and observing his finished work. Daniel Ellicott in Kandahar and Daniel Ellicott in Kansas City might be mirror images of one another, but the Apostle Paul said that what we see in a mirror we see only darkly. Your father placed high value on the importance of a face-to-face probe. Only then will you understand a man's vision and how that vision would translate into a blueprint for the Spire's future."

"Makes sense. I already know what your vision would involve. Immediate elimination of my theme park." Serenity settled back into the seat cushions and watched closely his reaction. The trip would be long, but much more enjoyable if she could provoke him into one of their intellectual skirmishes. Nothing pleased her more than the chance to play at jousting with words rather than lances.

Ben recognized the compression of her eyes and constriction of lips which signaled a thirst for conflict. Logical, or illogical, argument seemed to be their principle choice for conversation ever since the inception of the park project. Polemics provided a soccer pitch they both found gratifying. "I didn't realize you had acquired the ability to read minds," he countered.

"A closed mind can easily become an open book."

"An open book should easily satisfy the consternations of a closed mind. Does your insight into my vision pertain to viability, theology, or budgetary concerns?"

"Theology. Not even a closed mind could question the profitability and viability of the Spirit of the Spire."

"Agreed. Theology then. Specific venues or overall apprehensions?" He wanted to tell her how her entire countenance ignited in what he had come to describe as debate mode. Her eyes grew brighter, her ears reddened, her lips looked fuller. Even her hair seemed to stand on end like the hackles on a cat. She was never more beautiful than when she argued. Unable to share his heart, he instead took great satisfaction from their mental sparring.

"You've never camouflaged your distaste for the Bride of the Lamb Chapel and Peter's Fishing Pond."

"The first because it depreciates the value of the relationship between Christ and His church, and the second because Peter used nets rather than Zebco reels and canned corn."

"Paul chose to use marriage as his primary illustration of the intimacy between Christ and His bride, and 'Peter, James and John in a Sailboat' still qualifies as one of the greatest children's choruses ever composed. Let's discuss those initial worries you were so quick to share. How can you possibly conclude that experiencing the theme park destroys the impact of the biblical framework engendered by the teaching my father does in the Spire? Perhaps you don't understand how offensive I find that accusation."

Ben chuckled, which he knew only irritated her more. She hated to be called on her tendency toward exaggeration. "Had I made such an accusation you would be justified in your offense. It would have been an offensive remark. I grant you that, for most park visitors, a ride on Elijah's Chariot or a visit to Satan's Sanctuary involves nothing more than entertainment. Many have walked away with a greater appreciation for church history and a vivid impression of the reality of biblical events. A visit to the park imparts the background of biblical knowledge missing in the liberal educa-tion of modern man. You provide a virtual McGuffey's Reader for a new generation of non-readers."

"I'll take that as a compliment."

"You should. My hesitation stems from an observation by Marshall McLuhan at the rise of the social media age. He famously suggested that 'the medium is the message.' In the case of the theme park, I fear the medium conveys a false message, one which suggests that history can be rewritten."

"Never! You are absolutely wrong! I have made every effort to assure the accurate depiction of every historical event portrayed throughout the park. I can't believe you would suggest otherwise." Serenity grabbed a pil-low from the couch where she sat and playfully threw it across the plane in his direction. Ben caught it easily, thankful it had not been one of the dishes they had used at breakfast.

"Just hear me out. I am not questioning your historical accuracy. In fact, I admire the research which has contributed greatly to the overall veracity of each experience. The potential danger stems from repetition rather than authenticity. Take Descent into Hades for example. The first time a person drops through the surface of the earth and enters the under-world they encounter visual terror, auditory chaos, the smell of brimstone, a craving for relief from aridity, and the burning sensation of scorched skin. But they survive. Once back above ground their greatest desire focuses on repeating those sensations."

"I certainly hope so. Repeat ridership increases revenue."

Ben continued as if she had not interrupted. "Therein lies the rub. Having survived the underworld, they desire to return. But no one returns from death. Descent into Hades has generated a false hope. The hope that death can be survived."

"Nonsense. You might just as well argue that the desire to return stems from the hope that death is not the end. People simply want to celebrate their escape from Hades through the faith in God my father proclaims from the Spire pulpit. The rich man described by Jesus in Luke sixteen didn't want his brothers to join him."

Ben tried to avoid smiling his triumph as she contemplated what she had just said. "Thank you," he whispered. "My point exactly."

For the next several hours they bantered about the theme park and obscure theological questions, broken only by the sharing of meals and perusal of the material on Daniel Ellicott. Passing the file back and forth page by page, Serenity asked a question.

"By the way, do you speak either Dari or Pashto?"

Ben grinned. "I expect Daniel will provide all the translation work we need. We could use the Reversal of Babel app, but that would seem strange, talking on phones when we are in the same room. In addition to studying his file in order to plan your interview, I would recommend some sleep as well. Day and night will basically be reversed in our circadian rhythm when we arrive. Jet lag can be a real bear."

Ashley's promise of prime rib along with a brief refueling stop in Rome underscored the importance of dealing with jet lag on a fourteen-hour flight, even on a comfortable company aircraft. When they left Rome and the cabin lights dimmed, Serenity had no problem falling into a deep sleep. She was still groggy when Ashley's voice reminded them to fasten their seatbelts for landing.

Once on the ground Melvin opened the door while two airport workers maneuvered stairs into place outside. "We'll stay here with the plane and be ready to go whenever you give the word." He helped carry their luggage down the stairs and placed it on the runway before heading back up and closing the door.

Ben and Serenity looked around for a terminal. A series of Quonset hut type hangers to one side and domed windows overlooking a row of cement arches greeted them with a sense of military precision. A sign in Arabic and English, almost unreadable in the growing dusk, denoted a possible entrance. Uniformed men patrolled the area between them and the buildings while a mix of Soviet and American built tanks stood guard. Deciding to head for the doors under the sign, they started to pull their suitcases across the tarmac when suddenly a Toyota Land Cruiser raced toward them, blocking their way. From inside the vehicle three robed figures emerged. One of them threw a large wool blanket over Serenity's head and wrapped his arms around her upper body while a second man picked up her feet and placed her roughly into the back of the Toyota. Their suitcases were piled around her, and almost before she could catch her breath the doors slammed shut and the engine raced as they sped out of the airport.

# CHAPTER FIVE

T he ancient Land Cruiser careened around a corner toward a narrow road winding through the mountains between Kandahar and Lashkar Gah. Dangerous at any speed on a sunlit day, the road through town proved treacherous at night, without headlights. Ahmed, a young Afghan swathed in baggy white pants and an enormous white shirt with tails hanging free, drove carelessly. One hand stayed on the wheel, the other punctuated a running commentary on his favorite subject, his country's tenacity for survival.

"Tamerlane destroyed Kandahar in 1383. Built huge towers with the skulls of the people he executed. But Kandahar survives. Genghis Khan razed Balkh, Banian, Ghazni, and Herat. But the people melted into the mountains to return when he was gone. Three times we defeated the English. Twice the French, and then the Russians. The Americans came to rescue us from ourselves, but they are gone, and we remain."

Daniel Ellicott shifted in the seat beside Ahmed, pulling his sheepskin postin more closely around him. His years in Afghanistan had succeeded in thickening everything except his blood. The 17,000-foot peaks of the Koh-i-Bara, and the even taller Hindu Kush, insured a fairly decent chance of encountering snow on a trip through the countryside no matter what season of the year. Turning toward the two men in the seats behind him, he quickly translated Ahmed's comments into English as the driver rambled on.

"One-third of my people left for Pakistan, another group for Iran. The Russians used our boys for target practice, our fields for maneuvers, our students for conscripts, and our women for trash. The Americans destroyed

32

the economy by burning the opium fields and built schools so girls could study worthless subjects like Shakespeare and Gloria Steinem while listening to Jay-Z and Rihanna. Seldom did any of our liberators or conquerors control anything beyond the city limits of Kabul. But we survived. We are the remnants of triumph."

Dan grinned under his turban, wrapped tightly to cut the mountain chill. Ahmed demonstrated justifiable pride. No other nation on earth possessed such a record of tenacity in the face of foreign invasion. The cost had been great, but every Afghan knew that even the pullout of the American military had been, for the foreigners, a retreat and not a victory.

"Can we make Lashkar Gah in time for supper?"

"No problem," Ahmed punctuated his reply by pressing even heavier on the gas pedal. "I'll have you eating pomegranates, walnuts, pistachios, and almonds long before the mantu is ready to be served. Kabobs, eggplant, and spinach await. We will eat until the mullahs climb their minarets for morning prayers."

Serenity could hear muffled voices, even some English words, through her heavy covering. She didn't seem to be bound, although the suitcases piled around her held her tightly in place. The woolen blanket scratched as she shifted into a more comfortable position, quietly so as not to draw attention to her movements. Where was Ben? Had he also been captured? Where were they taking her? Why hadn't Daniel Ellicott been there to pick them up? She cautiously pulled the blanket off her head and raised herself in order to see her captors. As soon as her eyes lifted above the back of the seats, they caught the reflection of the driver's gaze in his rearview mirror. The car jerked and nearly spun out of control as he released his single-handed grip from the wheel and used both hands to gesture wildly in her direction, while at the same time shouting something unintelligible at the other occupants. Ben occupied the seat right in front of her along with a turbaned individual she thought she recognized from the airport attack. The man in the passenger seat had to be Daniel Ellicott. As she watched, he ripped off his headdress and threw it in her direction.

"Cover her up, Ben. What in the world does she think she's doing? How could you allow her to show up here in what she was wearing?"

Ben caught the kaffiyeh and turned around. He gently placed the scarf over her hair, covered the top of her head with the agal rope and pulled one end of the contraption over her mouth and nose, tucking it into the agal so that only her eyes could be seen. "Please, Serenity," he whispered, "don't cause more anger. We'll explain as soon as possible."

Cause more anger? Who did they think caused anger? She'd been kidnapped. Smothered. Treated like a piece of baggage. How dare he criticize what she was wearing. A turtle-neck sweater with long sleeves. Nothing immodest there. She pulled the offending material away from her face and glared at her host. "You listen to me, Daniel Ellicott."

Her words disappeared in the torrent of shouted verbiage from the driver, once again accompanied by erratic jerks on the wheel which threatened immediate doom.

"No. You listen to me Serenity Edwards," Ellicott shouted. "Cover your face immediately or I'll tell you exactly what Ahmed here is saying. He's never seen the uncovered visage of another woman with the exception of his mother and sisters, and you are embarrassing him beyond belief. You're not in Kansas anymore, and the quicker you realize that the better."

His words hurt worse than a slap across the face. Reluctantly replacing the cloth over her mouth and nose, she stared at the back of the man she had already come to dislike. The driver returned one hand to the wheel, regained control of the Land Cruiser, and resumed his travelogue, apparently for the benefit of Ben. Once back under cover she felt she had become invisible.

"St. Thomas visited here just fifteen years after Christ's crucifixion," she heard Daniel translate for the driver, whose verbosity had settled back into a running commentary punctuated with only one hand instead of two. "Our ancestor Gondophares converted to Christianity seven hundred years before the Muslims arrived with the Koran. We who now embrace the cross have not turned our backs on history and culture. Who has suffered more than the Afghan people? Who can better understand a God willing to die on their behalf? We have received the message of the suffering Savior with open hearts."

Their arrival in Lashkar Gah released Serenity from her uncomfortable ride with the luggage. At least they let her walk into the house instead of carrying her, although Ellicott insisted that she keep the blanket wrapped firmly around her. Once inside, a woman in a long black robe and scarf-covered face led her into a room which seemed to be cut out of stone. An ornate Turkish carpet covered most of the floor surrounded by colorful pillows propped against the walls. One entire end of the room featured an exquisite burgundy curtain decorated profusely with gold calligraphy. She could hear the murmur of men's voices on the other side of the curtain.

"Welcome to Afghanistan, Miss Edwards." Her hostess removed the niqab covering her mouth. Her smile of greeting encouraged Serenity to do the same.

"You're English."

"American actually. And knowing these men, you have experienced a traumatic introduction to Afghan life. Please accept my apologies. I desired to travel with them, but Mostafa preferred that I stay here and prepare for your arrival. You have met Mostafa?"

"I can't say that I have met anyone, really. Our departure was quite abrupt."

"Yes. He called to share with me the circumstances at the airport. Again, I apologize. My name is Marion and Mostafa is my husband. Please be seated and allow me to offer an explanation. The pillows are really quite comfortable once you get used to not having chairs. Or perhaps you would like to freshen up first. I forget how tiresome a trip it can be from the States. Should I show you to your room?"

Serenity nodded, anxious to throw off the scratchy wool blanket and change out of the clothes she had now worn for almost two days. Marion led her to a small room with a single bed, a sink, and more pillows. Her suitcases lay on the floor against one wall.

"The meal will be served soon, but at least you will have time to change. I will bring you a robe and hijab to replace the blanket and kaffiyeh. You will find them much more comfortable."

Serenity opened her mouth to protest but remembered Ellicott's strong rebuke.

"They will be necessary, I assure you," Marion continued as she backed out of the room.

Muted conversation drew Serenity back into the first room she had seen after washing up, changing, and trying to figure out how to wear the floor-length robe, scarf, and niqab Marion left with her. Several women and young girls sat in a circle around the edge of the Persian carpet along with two small boys. The women and girls wore hijabs similar to the one she had donned, although their faces were uncovered. The boys' attire consisted of loose-fitting baggy pants, embroidered waistcoats, and short vests. The floor in front of them contained several large platters of food. Serenity recognized the rice and some sort of kabobs. The rest of the meat and vegetable dishes looked delicious, although she had no idea what they contained.

Marion rose to her feet, helped Serenity remove the niqab she had struggled to get into place, and gave her a kiss on one cheek while clasping both her hands in greeting. "Our guest tonight has come all the way from the United States to share in our meal," she said to the rest of the women, speaking first in English and then translating her words into Pashto. "Her name is Miss Edwards." Still holding Serenity's hand, she pulled her gently down into the circle. That seemed to mark the start of the festivities as platters were handed from person to person and food was scooped up by hand and deposited on plates in front of each guest.

"Borani kadoo," Marion announced as the first dish came past. "Squash with onions, garlic, chili peppers, and tomatoes, garnished with coriander and ginger. You will find it quite delicious."

Serenity looked around for silverware and realized quickly that hands must be the preferred utensils. She scooped borani kadoo onto her plate and added a piece of naan bread, something else she recognized.

"Mastawa." The next platter obviously contained rice, but also a mixture of meat and vegetables. "You would call it sticky rice. Chick-peas, sun-dried mutton, and quroot, Afghanistani cheese made from yogurt. The flavor comes from the bitter orange peels and hot peppers. I trust you will not find it too spicy. I still remember my first few meals when Mostafa took me to meet his parents. You will want to keep your cup filled with dough, a yogurt drink which helps to neutralize some of the stronger peppers."

The kabobs had been made with lamb. Dessert came in the form of elephant's ear, which Marion called Gosh-e fil, a sweet pastry with sugary icing, powdered cardamom, and crushed pistachios. The subdued voices of the women contrasted with the more boisterous conversation taking place on the other side of the curtain. The men in the house enjoyed a similar meal in their own room. When all had eaten their fill, washed down in Serenity's case with plenty of the yogurt drink, the food was removed. Each of the women covered her nose and mouth with a niqab, and Marion pulled back the curtain separating them from where the men had been eating. None of the men turned to look at them, and once again Serenity had the uncomfortable feeling that she and the others had become invisible.

Daniel Ellicott stood at the front of the room, Ben at his side. He seemed to be introducing Ben to the half-dozen men seated on pillows.

Only when Ben began to talk, punctuated by Ellicott's translation, did she realize that this was a worship service and Ben was bringing the message.

"I bring you greetings from the church in America, with all the believers in Christ Jesus our Lord. Grace and peace to you from God the Father, the Father of mercies and God of all comfort."

For the next half-hour he spoke in a conversational tone, pausing for the translation at short intervals and then continuing the thought as though he had not been interrupted.

He sounds so much like my father, Serenity thought. She noted how the casual, relaxed style which had proved so successful for Dr. Edwards over the years was mirrored in his assistant. Even though they can't understand the words, they listen just as closely to what he is saying as they do to the translation. Why hadn't her father included him on the list of potential successors? There must be something in his background which disqualified him from inclusion in T-3. She mentally reviewed the requirements Paul listed, trying to identify anything which might be lacking in Ben. His conduct toward her and others had always been above reproach. He treated her like a sister instead of like a woman. In fact, that was one of the qualities that irritated her, if she came right down to it. She had tried in a variety of ways to get him to notice her since returning from college, and nothing worked. Everyone on staff in the ministry spoke highly of him. Hospitality? He knew the names of all his co-workers. No question about his ability to teach. The only negative she could list came from the phrase "not quarrelsome." They argued a lot, but even then, he never grew violent, not even testy. One translation used the word "brawler," and that certainly could never be used to describe him. In her mind Ben fit the Timothy Three pattern perfectly. Perhaps father had determined to steer the ship in a different direction for the future. If he wanted Benjamin Morris to replace him, all he had to do was turn the speaking platform over to him. He had to have a reason for not doing that. Her father always had a reason. Lost in her thoughts, the end of the teaching session came as a surprise. Ben and Daniel rejoined the circle to answer questions the men seemed anxious to voice. Marion curtained the females off from the male conversation, and the women removed their face coverings.

"Perhaps some of you have questions for our guest, the daughter of Dr. Edwards who we listen to each Sunday." Marion patted Serenity's hand as if to show the women she would be willing to respond to anything they might wish to ask. The silence revealed a reluctance which Serenity could certainly understand. A silence for which she gave thanks, since she hadn't listened to Ben's lesson at all. What answers could she possibly have for a group of women she didn't know living half-way around the world?

Sensing hesitancy on the part of both her guest and the women gathered in the room, Marion changed tactics. "No questions? Then it must be time for us to get better acquainted. You have met our guest, please allow me to introduce each of you to her. Benesh and Damsa, my daughters."

Two of the younger women stood and approached Serenity with downcast eyes, leaning over to place a kiss on her cheeks before resuming their seats. "Benesh has been promised to Ahmed who you met earlier today. They will marry in the fall."

"Ah yes. Our driver. A very talented driver, Benesh." Serenity smiled, pleased to see a corresponding delight in the girl's eyes as her mother translated.

"Farahnoush and Gulnoor are the wives of Pazir, another of our guests this evening. The boys belong to them."

Like the sisters, the two women greeted her with a kiss. The boys sat quietly together on a pillow as they had done the entire evening.

"The other young man who has graced us with his presence this evening carries the name of the biblical Moses, Musa. Damsa, I believe has had her eye on him for some time, but my youngest daughter is still my baby and therefore I seek to discourage her from such hopes. But he is a fine young man." This time the eyes of the younger girl reflected the delight she took in her mother's gentle teasing, revealing an understanding of the English words even before any restatement.

"Do you meet often for such times of worship?" The responsibility entrusted to her by her father, as well as her own curiosity compelled Serenity to seek answers concerning Daniel Ellicott's ministry, even if his treatment of her had already poisoned her mind against his personal qualifications.

"Every Sunday, and once again during the week for a fellowship meal. Daniel cannot always be with us, but the miracle of technology provides access to the services from the Spire by means of our cell phones. Our small group assembly owes much to the excellent teaching from your father and Dr. Morris. When Daniel comes the men ply him with all the questions raised in their minds by the exposition of the word."

Noises from the other side of the curtain alerted them to the imminent departure of their guests. Farahnoush and Gulnoor replaced their niqabs and joined their husband after saying their farewells. Marion's daughters stayed on their own side of the room, faces covered, but eyes saying good-bye to Ahmed and Musa. When all the guests had left, Mustafa, Daniel, and Ben joined them in the women's living room. The daughters excused themselves and departed for another part of the house.

Daniel approached Serenity, placed his hand over his heart and bowed slightly. "Miss Edwards, I feel I must apologize for my conduct at the airport. Perhaps Marion has had an opportunity to share the perfect storm of circumstance which led to my behavior?"

"Certainly not. We have eaten, listened, and been for the most part ignored since we arrived. When has she had time to explain? Why should it be her responsibility to apologize for you?" As if to emphasize her ire, Serenity pulled the niqab off the lower part of her face. Mostafa immediately turned and left the room.

"Let me assure you that you have not been ignored. That has indeed been the problem from the beginning. You attracted the attention of every man in the entire airport complex. Guards were on the way to arrest you. The only way we could prevent that involved covering you completely and removing you from their sight. As much as I regret that necessity, the alternative would have been appealing to the embassy in Kabul for a visit from the American ambassador to personally plead for your release from prison. The last time that became unavoidable the negotiations took thirteen months."

Serenity glanced at Marion. "Just because I wasn't wearing a scarf?"

"Please excuse us, gentlemen," said Marion. "Culture shock here in our country remains very gender specific. I will try my best to explain, but for now, Mr. Ellicott, your presence will only tend to aggravate the situation further. Please allow me to handle this."

As Daniel and Ben left the room, Marion directed Serenity back to the bedroom where she had prepared for the evening meal. Sitting down on pillows, they both accepted steaming hot cups of tea from Benesa who bowed slightly and disappeared.

"Do you realize what they did, Marion? They wrapped me in a dirty blanket and threw me into the back of that vehicle like a piece of baggage. With the luggage, mind you."

Marion blew across the top of her cup and took a small sip before responding. "The first time I met Mostafa I had come to his parent's home to provide medical help to his mother. Doctors at the military hospital where I worked made sure I wore the hijab. Even so, I was not allowed to talk to his mother directly. I would ask questions of the husband. He would address his wife. The wife would reply and then the husband would tell me what she said. This was not translation, you understand. I could speak Pashto fluently, could understand his remarks to her as well as her answers to him, but could not speak to her directly. The culture forbad it."

"But all of those here tonight were believers. Surely such nonsense no longer remains necessary. You spoke to these women directly."

"Because they are believers, yes. Some changes have occurred. But we are also Afghans. As difficult as it may be for you to understand, we continue to dress in the cultural style of our people because we love them. You offended my husband tonight by uncovering your face. I can understand your action and forgive you for something you never intended to do. But the fact remains that he was so offended he had to leave the room. Ahmed had never seen a woman's face, with the exception of his mother and sisters, before you showed up at the airport tonight. You shocked him, and the word he used which drove Daniel Ellicott to such immediate action was 'naked.' If that was the way Ahmed saw you, just imagine what happened in the minds of the workmen and guards who were seeing not only a woman's mouth and nose, but her neck and her hair."

Serenity slumped down into the pillow, weary from the travel as well as the awareness of what she had done. "I am truly sorry to have offended Mustafa. Please forgive me. I am more than willing to give up my freedom in order to make possible my continued visit to your country."

"Ah, but we do not give up our freedom by wearing the hijab. We gain it. Sleep well, Miss Edwards. Perhaps tomorrow you will understand."

# Chapter Six

Three days later Serenity thought she might be understanding what Marion meant by the freedom of the hijab. When they entered and left each village, Daniel and Ben faced questions at the guard posts, with Ben carrying his passport constantly for identification. She was simply ignored, treated as though invisible. Her clothing provided freedom from all restrictions on travel. Once covered completely she ceased to exist to the men.

Within the village homes her reception could not have been of greater contrast. The women greeted her, fed her, questioned her, and shared grateful testimonies concerning the impact her father's messages had on their lives. They sat quietly in separate groups while Ben spoke and Daniel translated. Once the curtain closed and the murmurs of men's voices faded into the distance, she found herself surrounded by friendly faces curious about America, but even more inquisitive about spiritual matters—prayer, thanksgiving, fasting, confession, and worship. Not once had she been asked about dress.

"It's not an issue," Daniel had assumed the driving responsibilities for Ahmed for these trips and drove almost as recklessly through the hills and mountains. "It's a way of life and a matter of modesty. After all, the Bible has much to say about modesty. Who fits that description better? The women you have met over the past few days or the average teen-age girl in an American church on Sunday morning?"

She still had not learned to appreciate his blunt manner which she felt bordered on rudeness. But three days of travel through western Afghanistan had increased her respect for the work he had accomplished. In multiple villages they had met with small groups in homes, never more than twelve to fifteen, but all anxious to hear a lesson from Ben and then take the opportunity to pepper Daniel with spiritual questions. He had mentioned almost casually that such gatherings took place in more than fifteen hundred Afghan locations on a weekly basis. He had never even been in many of the homes. In order to allay suspicion on the part of the mullahs, any group which grew to more than sixteen immediately divided in half and met separately. His visits were kept to a minimum in order to assuage fears of reprisal.

"But doesn't this exaggerated sense of modesty on the part of the men stem from a desire to control women, to make them less than human? How can you say it is just cultural when it clearly comes from religious roots as well? Doesn't the Bible say that the truth will set us free?"

"What in your mind has greater importance?" said Daniel. "To be set free from condemnation or to be set free from cultural mores? If these women who have come to believe in God would suddenly throw off centuries of cultural practice in order to dress like Americans, our home gatherings would cease to exist. Local government authorities would close us down faster than this Land Rover can go from one to sixty."

"But only the women have to hide," she protested. "Where's the freedom in that?"

Ben forced himself to take his eyes off the road and trust the driving to his companion. "Sere, do you remember when the Covid-19 pandemic hit and the Centers for Disease Control recommended masks and social distancing? Some governors mandated the masks and others didn't. But social pressure, peer pressure, took over. If you wanted to go shopping, or enter a restaurant, or even go to church, you put on a mask. In essence, the mask set you free. Many people hated the masks and resented the governmental interference, but if they wanted to be free to move about in society they wore the masks, a cultural mandate."

"So, women here in Afghanistan are condemned to a lifetime of second-class citizenship because of a government mandate which no one likes? If you were to succeed my father, Mr. Ellicott, would this cultural mandate be advocated for churches in America as well?"

Daniel pulled to the side of the road in front of another small dwelling. "I guess that is something we will never know since I have no intention of leaving Afghanistan."

The house at the edge of the village of Bala Boluk appeared to be one of the smallest homes they had yet visited. Ten women and girls crowded the walls of the living space, sliding together to make room for Serenity to sit. Just two men greeted Ben and Daniel on the other side of the room before the lesson began. Since none of the women spoke English, Serenity communicated through smiles and nods during the refreshment time, giving thanks for what looked like a variety of nuts and raisins with orange peel and rice. The mixture proved delicious.

She replaced her niqab carefully once they had eaten and the curtain had been removed. Daniel introduced her to Ebrahim and Kardaar who in turn shared the names of each of the women and girls. Farewells consisted of smiles and nods, and once again they were on their way in the Land Rover.

The road wound up the side of a steep mountain. Although Ben sat on the inside against the cliff, he still tensed up around every corner, certain that a truck coming from above would not find room to pass them on the narrow trail. Serenity removed her face covering, the niqab, in order to make breathing easier. She knew she would never be able to adapt to wearing it constantly. Something even more distressing began to occupy her thoughts. She remembered Farahnoush and Gulnoor, the wives of Pazir she had met in the house of Marion. Then Ebrahim and Kardaar with all those women. They had to be wives, at least some of them. Could she possibly recommend someone to the InSpire Ministries who believed in polygamy? Daniel's abrupt announcement that he didn't intend to leave Afghanistan was undoubtedly for the best. It certainly made her decision easier.

"What would you say is your greatest challenge?" She heard Ben pose the question to Daniel. "Your home study groups seem to be flying under the radar of the village mullahs. Almost like the underground in Nazi occupied France during World War II."

"We've tried hard not to stir the waters. Most religion, as you know, involves externalism. If looks conform to preconceptions, inner motivations and even beliefs are ignored. Most Americans think anyone who gets married or buried in church believes in God. The external rituals mask the tragedy of empty hearts. Externalism has worked to our advantage here in Afghanistan. Transformed hearts cannot be seen by those whose only concern remains outward appearance."

"So you teach them to hide their faith?" Serenity leaned forward to remind the men of her involvement. Sometimes even Ben seemed to ignore her, which wasn't new, but still aggravating. She couldn't even manage to engage him in a decent argument since their arrival. Instead he delegated that responsibility to Daniel. "That doesn't sound very transformative."

"Hide their faith? Not at all. Love cannot be hidden. Joy shines through even if only the eyes can be seen. A peaceful home life draws attention and prompts inquiry. A gentle spirit replacing bitterness and anger glows in a small village like a campfire on a cloudless night. Evil deeds will be whispered, but goodness shouts. The flag of self-control stands out like a banner in an army of the unrestrained. Hide their faith? These believers trumpet their faith constantly. Conforming to dress standards does not hide their faith, it makes possible the greatest display of that faith."

"Are you saying a transformed inner man excuses all external behavior? As long as you are thinking right, it makes no difference what you do? Heart belief makes outward change unnecessary. Tell that to St. James. Faith without works is dead."

Ben turned to look at her. She had been so different since their arrival. It was unlike her to demonstrate such hostility. Deliberate misunderstanding had never characterized her style. "He didn't say that, Sere. You've met these people. They are gracious, kind, and hospitable. Daniel's reference to externalism involves matters of dress, which you must admit are not immodest."

"What about polygamy?" she interrupted. "You probably haven't even noticed it, Benjamin Morris, since females all become invisible behind these ridiculous costumes. But every place we've been the women outnumber the men. Having more than one wife apparently doesn't matter to Mr. Ellicott's theology as long as men's hearts are changed. Where is the love in that? Where is your shouted goodness? Where is the banner of self-control? Dragging in the mud, that's where it is."

The approach of another vehicle careening down the trail in their direction brought Ben's attention back to the front. Daniel squeezed the Rover as far to right as possible without scraping paint off the door handles, concentrating on survival with a carelessness born of long drives through dangerous territory.

"Guilty as charged," he said, slowing briefly as the other car passed them and then resuming his previous speed. The three of them gazed out at the landscape in brittle silence. The snow-covered Hindu Kush rose forbiddingly in the distance framing a series of lesser peaks with valleys like playground slides dropping off into the deserts. A royal blue sky, empty of clouds, promised another scorcher for those living in the valleys. The vast area spread out before them seemed endless, as if all the world lay open to their view. The expanse of the panorama seemed to lend sweeping import to the words offered by the missionary.

"Sometimes I feel Afghanistan exists in the days of Abraham, Moses, and David. As if some time traveler handed a cell phone to Jacob, inviting him to listen to a message from Dr. Ernst Edwards delivered four thousand years in the future. Jacob listens, knows the message comes from God, and turns to me for answers to questions more complex than any I have ever before encountered. 'I have more than one wife,' he says to me. 'What am I to do with this message from the Apostle Paul?' So, we talk, and talk, and talk. Should he send all but one of the wives away? If so, which one should stay? The oldest? The one who has given him the most children? Where will he send them? Back to the houses of their fathers who are not believers and would marry them off to husbands who have no faith?"

The country even looks like the Old Testament, thought Serenity. Daniel resembled a prophet with his full beard and kaffiyeh, his ancient eyes that sometimes glowed with the same passion she could imagine in an Isaiah. The hijab question had been personal, selfish even, she was willing to admit. She could fly back to a country where face scarves served only as accessories. He lived among those whose discovery of faith carried them four thousand years into the future without the privilege of gradual historical developments.

"Mostafa will not take another wife in addition to Marion. When Ahmed marries Benesh she will be his only wife. Perhaps in another generation the questions will be answered, perhaps it will take four thousand years. But in the meantime, we live with reality. David, the polygamist, could still be a man after God's own heart. Paul, the murderer, could find forgiveness even though those he killed could not be restored to life."

Before them the sweeping perspective of the Afghan landscape revealed a vista virtually untouched and unexplored. Having briefly glimpsed the spiritual perspective through the eyes of Daniel Ellicott, she knew he would never flourish in Kansas City. He was a man sent from God to Afghanistan.

## CHAPTER SEVEN

"You love her." Daniel glanced into the mirror of the Land Rover to make certain Serenity still slept soundly on the back seat. He had chosen to drive them back to Kandahar rather than trusting Ahmed to keep his eyes on the road as they bounced over the narrow trails.

Ben looked back as well before replying. "Always have. Is it that obvious?"

"Marion told me first, but I would have seen it eventually. She doesn't know?"

"It's better that way, especially with this convoluted path to succession her father arranged. She doesn't realize that I'm on the list."

"Dr. Edwards cooked it up to bring you together. He wants her to look at each of us so she will realize that you are the one she needs."

"Sounds really bizarre when you frame it that way, but that remains a distinct possibility. Not that he ever admitted complicity or ordered me to marry her or anything like that. He wants both of us to be free to choose."

"But you don't think she would see it that way?"

"Bingo. You've only known her three days and you can already guess her reaction. If there were even a hint of collusion between me and her father, the fireworks would rival the New Year celebration in Sydney."

"How did you keep it from her?"

"I didn't. Dr. Edwards gave the files to the company lawyer and had him explain the plan. When we flew out of Kansas City, she shared three dossiers instead of four. At first, I thought she had already crossed me off the list out of vexation with both me and her father. The longer we talked the more I realized that she had only been given three files—yours, DeLoran's and Wilson's. I need to ask Ernst what happened. It won't be pretty if he introduces me as another option late in the process."

"Why not just tell her? She knows you were involved in generating T-3. She'll assume immediately that someone has kept the truth from her on purpose. Why risk that?" Daniel swerved into the left lane to pass a slow-moving cattle truck and then maneuvered ahead of it to avoid an on-coming donkey cart. "That still remains my frustration with all those Shakespeare plays we read in literature class. Why didn't they just talk? Romeo and Juliet. Benedict and Beatrice. Othello and Desdemona. Think of all the drawn-out death scenes which could have been avoided. Just talk."

"Unintended consequences. Imagine what would have happened to Romeo if he had been discovered alive in that tomb with Juliet lying dead on the slab? They would have accused him of murder. It made a much better story for her to try to kill herself by kissing the poison from his lips. At least this provides me with an opportunity to spend time with her apart from any pressure from her father. Maybe…"

"Maybe what? There's something more here than just playing a part in some drama. I can't see where this 'I loved you once in silence' act benefits you any more than it did Lancelot. You've never shied away from any other challenge."

"Long story," muttered Ben.

"Long journey," answered Daniel.

For the next several minutes Dan drove in silence as he listened to a story few knew concerning Benjamin Morris. His mother Ricci enrolled in the MFA program for creative writing at Enderson College after showing great potential in undergrad classes in her home state university system. Midway through her junior year she found herself with child after a brief affair with one of the professors. Instead of approaching him with the news, she dropped out of school, never telling him about the birth of her son, Benjamin. She raised him as a single mother while working odd jobs and completing a series of novels without any success at finding a publisher.

Benjamin taught himself to read at age three. His mother exposed him to short children's films and cartoons in French and soon realized that languages came easily for her son. One Sunday morning as they were watching the service from the Spire, he heard Dr. Edwards mention Greek. The idea of reading God's word in the language in which it had been written fascinated him, and by the time he was ten he had mastered both Greek and Hebrew. His home-school curriculum led to a high school diploma at fourteen. His first online college degree was granted at seventeen. He completed one doctoral degree at twenty and had nearly completed a second when he moved to Kansas City at the invitation of Dr. Edwards, who had offered to mentor him. His first glimpse of Serenity came when she waved goodbye and drove off for her freshman year of college, but the impression had been made. An image of her face had been forever etched on the surface of his cortex.

"My early success at education and extensive online learning definitely impeded my social progress while accelerating my scholastic achievements. I knew how to say "I love you" in seven languages but have never had the courage to express those words in English to Serenity Edwards. It was good she was away most of the next four years. Her intermittent visits provided time for us to establish a friendship, but nothing more."

"Because you wouldn't risk it." Daniel laughed softly. "You may be the smartest individual I have ever met. And one of the dumbest. Letters? Phone calls? Texts? Instagram? Flowers? Poetry? Visits to campus? Dinner for two? Have you tried anything?"

"I doubt my ability to make you understand, since you enjoyed a normal upbringing. The risk outweighs the venture. I don't know my father."

Daniel took his eyes off the road and stared at his friend in amazement. "And so?"

"That one fact elevates the risk factor to the realm of impossibility."

"You lost me there with your brilliance, Morris. Not knowing who fathered you makes it impossible for you to woo the woman of your dreams? What kind of hereditary nonsense have you espoused? Divine right of kings?"

"There's more to the story. After I had worked with Dr. Edwards for about six months, my mother came to visit. The boss has this knack for setting people at ease just like he does during his messages. When he learned that she had written a novel about a space traveler who encounters a totally alien culture and seeks for ways to communicate the gospel without knowing for certain if the creatures even possess souls, he asked to read it. Before long he had funded the publication of the book as a Freedom Project. That book and the series which followed have now sold over a million copies."

"Ric Morris. I should have known. So your mother has achieved success beyond imagination, your father remains invisible, and romance proves impossible. I admire the way your mind works, but the labyrinthine trails have succeeded in losing me completely."

"Alright then, hear this. Dr. Edwards could be my father. Serenity could be my sister."

"Because he funded your mother for a Freedom Project? How many other times has he done that? My work here in Afghanistan has been a Freedom Project. Hardly a week goes by without another recipient of his encouragement toward creativity sharing his or her story. The artist who painted those amazing murals depicting the attributes of an invisible God, the couple who established the Biblical Hall of Fame Wax Museum, the musical creations of Michal DeLoran, Serenity's own Spirit of the Spire. The list is practically endless."

"The timing is right. Dr. Edwards would still have been single when I was born."

"And you're going to tell me that he was teaching at Enderson College when your mother was a student?"

"No nothing like that. And I would never suggest that he would be capable of seducing an undergraduate. Not in a million years. But mother won't talk about it. She says it was a professor, but that's all she'll say. I don't know. He could be anyone. A socialist. A free-thinker. An atheist. A murderer. How could I possibly ask someone to marry me when I don't know my own genetic pool?"

Daniel had heard enough. Shaking his head in disbelief at the thought that a man could be so wise and so stupid simultaneously, he practically shouted to make his point. "And you're going to allow something you don't know to ruin your future? What about grace? Forgiveness? Personal sanctification? Go talk to your mother. Find out the truth. Don't be an idiot."

"Who's an idiot," came the voice from the back seat.

Ben clamped down hard on Dan's arm to warn him against answering and gave Serenity what he hoped was a sincere smile. "Did you sleep well?"

"Until you two started yelling at each other. How long did I sleep?"

Not long enough thought Ben, wondering how much of their conversation she might have overheard.

"At least an hour," said Daniel. "Another forty-five minutes and we'll have you back on your plane. Fourteen more hours and you'll be comfortable in your own bed."

"Not yet," said Ben. "The Prophet will be in concert at Red Rocks Amphitheater tomorrow night. We can't miss his performance."

Serenity rubbed the sleep from her eyes and leaned forward to watch the road. "Daniel, I want to apologize for getting off on the wrong foot. I have come to greatly appreciate your ministry and I can certainly understand your hesitation about leaving Afghanistan. But if you were to take my father's place at the Spire, what would you want to see happen?"

"I've thought about that ever since your father called to say that you would be coming." He slowed down to a crawl behind a horse-drawn wagon, waiting for an opportunity to pass. "I can really answer that only in terms of the work here, but I think there are some ideas which would apply to many other places in the world as well. The western world has enjoyed almost two thousand years of biblical inculcation. Not that everyone there believes the Bible—far from it. But western literature depends heavily on biblical themes. I remember a lecturer in college listing over fifty allusions to scripture in Othello alone. Merchant of Venice has Shylock lauding 'a Daniel come to judgement,' and Warwick in Henry VI orders the head of his enemy to be displayed on the gates of York by paraphrasing Matthew 7:2, 'measure for measure must be answered.'"

"The sons of Edward sleep in Abraham's bosom," quoted Ben.

"I'll go sleep if I can; if I cannot, I'll rail against all the first-born of Egypt," added Serenity.

"Guess we all heard similar lectures," laughed Dan. "Although I think both of you have sleep on the brain. Anyway, Afghanistan doesn't have the privilege of those years of biblical influence on literature. Our legal system stems from the Koran instead of the law of Moses. The treatment of women, which you have found so offensive, remains ingrained in the very fabric of our society. We need those who can study the Bible and become house church pastors. But they will need tools, and those tools cannot just be translated from English. We need indigenous biblical scholars. It will not be enough to provide Pashto and Dari versions of C. S. Lewis. We need men and women who write Inklings-worthy books from the Afghan perspective."

"It could be done," said Serenity. "The same technology which translates father's messages into all those languages could make it possible."

"We've actually talked about it." Ben's usually quiet tones rose in pitch as he grew excited. "Dr. Edwards and I. We could develop classes taught by nationals, or by those like Dan who think like nationals. Offer the courses free, even grant degrees. It could be the largest on-line university system in the world since we already reach over one hundred and eighty different language groups. Not just Bible courses, but creative writing and nursing, business and communications, finance, pharmacology, computer science, engineering, education, psychology, the list goes on. All from a biblical worldview."

"Our people here in Afghanistan listen to your father and are changed by what they hear from the word of God. I know they would also listen to professors sponsored by the Spire. That type of universal learning could bring about a paradigm shift in just one generation. You need to do it, Ben."

He was right. Serenity knew he was right. But Benjamin Morris had not appeared on the list of those her father deemed worthy of succession. He had not been chosen as part of T-3. According to her father, Ben did not meet the qualifications which the Apostle Paul considered basic for ministerial success. What did he lack? As long as she had known him, he had been above reproach. She had never heard anyone blame him of wrongdoing. His teaching skills mirrored and perhaps even exceeded those of her father. Patient? His name could be used as an illustration of that quality in a dictionary. Gentle? Not quarrelsome? Self-controlled? In comparison to her temper, Ben should be nominated for a Nobel Peace Prize.

As she racked her brain to think of whatever could have disqualified him in the mind of her father, Dan drove onto the tarmac and stopped at the end of the Gulfstream access steps.

"Nice outfit," joked Ashley as she greeted them at the top of the stairs. "Actually, I could have used a full hijab myself. Melvin and I had to fly to Mumbai to find a place to stay and something to eat. They wouldn't let me off the plane here in Kandahar."

"Freedom," smiled Serenity. "The truth will make you free."

# CHAPTER EIGHT

Thousands of hands alternated between applauding and jabbing "one way" fingers into the sky over the Red Rock Amphitheater above Denver. Many had already waited for hours in the fading heat, their enthusiasm building as the time of arrival drew near. Already the clear crystal stage diffused with rainbow hues shook with the rhythm of the opening act, drumming out a heavy metal version of "When the Saints Go Marching In."

Without warning, green and blue spotlights crisscrossed the sky in search of the distant noise of a helicopter. The tempo of the clapping hands increased as eyes turned heavenward, searching for the first glimpse of their musical idol. The "one way" fingers ceased jabbing and steadied, focused on the spotlights. Gradually the Altman ellipsoidals converged on a figure all in white, suspended in midair from the underside of a Chinook CH-47.

"Prophet! Prophet! Prophet!" The entire crowd screamed, pointed, danced in place. The rope and harness, all but invisible in the rapidly growing dusk, allowed him to descend slowly from the clouds to the rainbow infused stage. As his feet touched the platform, the sound of an explosion rocked the mountainside. Clouds of white smoke billowed from below the crystal dais. Lights flickered and dimmed. From out of the darkness a thundering voice, amplified almost to the point of distortion, boomed, "Behold he comes! And every eye shall see him."

As the voice echoed and re-echoed into oblivion on the distant crags of the Rocky Mountains, a phalanx of blue lights illuminated the stage. A solitary figure arrayed in white tights and a silk body vest appeared, arms extended in the shape of a cross, head bent back almost parallel to the ground. A staccato of percussion beats slowly straightened his back until, once upright, he erupted in a stiff legged, sky-reaching jump and came down with a silver microphone in his hand.

The concert which followed satisfied even those who had paid three hundred dollars for a scalped ticket granting them a seat on the red rock bleachers. Racing from side to side on the crystal lake, sliding on his back or stomach, rolling over and over, he never missed a beat with his guttural, hard-driving, high-pitched vocals. Pure dynamite. Capable of a phenomenal range of sound, he thrilled, teased, manipulated, and stroked the audience until assuming total possession of their minds and souls.

Notwithstanding the huge crowd, security remained almost nonexistent. A new day had arisen in contemporary music. Acid trips replaced by spiritual journeys, arrests for possession unknown. There had been an incident in Pekin, Illinois, where a conscientious objector with a picket sign had been forcibly removed. But no one expected trouble when the Prophet came to town. The entertainment scene had entered a new era. Youth tuned in, turned on—high on religion.

Two solid hours of uplifting, energizing, passionate performance. Each rendition a favorite, each more powerful than the last. Serenity had heard the Prophet before, but never in person. You couldn't walk through a mall anywhere in the country without seeing his image on multiple screens. She knew exactly when the chord progressions transitioned and the finale began.

"Coming Again," the video which catapulted the Prophet to national prominence, still highlighted the climax of each appearance. Having long since gone platinum, it remained on the charts longer than any single in recording industry history. Defenders of the Prophet's approach to musical evangelism hailed it as positive evidence of religious revival among the youth of America.

"Coming Again" delivered more than just a song; it provided an experience. Red lights from below the crystal platform created an inferno through which frenetic demons with bright red guitars pranced in choreographed disarray. A scrim heightened the sensual effect of their gyrations, capturing them in seeming bondage as they struggled against the cloth separating them from freedom. Soulful, minor harmonies with rhythmic heavy metal overtones reflected the almost total obsession of rock and rap with evil in the pre-Prophet era.

Satan. Master Satan.

Dance with me. Dance with me.

Grateful master of depression.

Hateful master of obsession.

Fateful master of possession.

Master. Master. Master Satan.

Dance with me.

Even though she had seen the video countless times, it had not prepared her for the impact of the presentation when experiencing it firsthand. Glancing over at Ben to see his reaction, she allowed herself a slight smile. From the look on his face, he had never even watched the video. His eyes flickered pell-mell across the scene, gaping as countless gruesome images of man's inhumanity to man appeared in fleeting montage. Heads rolled from seventeenth-century guillotines and exploded into twentieth-century mushroom clouds. Swastika-banded guards presided over Buchenwald ovens which faded into antiseptic hospital disposal bags overflowing with aborted fetuses. Garish lights of pornographic advertising morphed into the dismembered bodies of victims of sexual exploitation by nameless serial murderers. Above the images throbbed the pulsating beat of "Master Satan."

Like frontier crowds at a melodrama, the crowd booed and hissed every time Satan's name materialized from the lyrics. Anticipation grew. No matter how long the beat of "Master Satan" continued, they knew he was "Coming Again."

And come he did.

Transfiguration. Serenity almost caught herself saying it aloud. The only word to describe the dramatic change. A single light from nowhere, arising abruptly from the extreme edge of the craggy rocks behind them, cut through the red clouds, transfixing the white, silk-clad figure which, without warning, had appeared in the midst of the demons.

"Coming!" The triumphant tones in the guttural voice of the Prophet eclipsed the driving beat of "Master Satan." The light from nowhere began to spread.

"Coming!" One voice in control. One sound to dominate. The crowd began to murmur an approving response.

"Coming!" He teased them with a dash toward a red-clad demon.

"Coming!" They thrilled to a brilliantly lit slide through the red inferno, spreading white flames in a jet stream behind him.

"Coming! Coming! Coming!" For nearly seven minutes that word repeated, with each occurrence reaching a new level of excitement. Crowds of youth climbed onto the benches, cheering wildly every time the white light transformed another demon and guitar into a worshipping angel. The scrim disappeared. Performers blended with the front rows of the audience. Fingers and fists clawed the heavens in unison as the crescendo of percussion and synthesizers accompanied the amplified shouts of the Prophet to an insurmountable peak.

When it seemed as if another decibel of sound would literally split the earth in two, everything fell silent. Serenity knew what was coming, yet in the surprise of the moment gasped to hear the beat of her own blood drumming against her temples. Amidst the orchestrated silence, the Prophet inaugurated a solitary dance of coronation. In theological terms he portrayed the awesome hush when universal worship engulfs the totality of humankind. In fiscal terms, he delivered the most profitable thirty seconds of silence in music history. Bodies strained, seeking vicariously to assimilate his every move. The massive crowd moved as one, falling to their knees and joining their voices in one tremendous shout which echoed off the rocks and seemed to move the mountains themselves.

"LORD!"

# CHAPTER NINE

T he ordinary ranch-style rambler in a middle-class neighborhood of Broomfield did not fit the image of a residence Serenity would have imagined for the Prophet. The man who opened the door for her and Ben represented an even greater surprise. The showman on stage at Red Rocks had appeared to be well over six feet tall. This man stood even shorter than her five ten in heels. Videos of "Coming" included close-up shots of a clean-shaven face framed by blond hair with a definite curl covering his ears. The man greeting them with a broad smile of welcome had straight hair, light brown but certainly not blond, and cut in almost a military style. A well-trimmed mustache and beard, which certainly could not have been grown since the concert the night before, covered the lower part of an otherwise undistinguished face.

"Michal DeLoran," he said as he extended a hand to each of them in turn. "And to answer the unvoiced question, no, I am not the Prophet."

Serenity's mind raced back over the information her father had provided in the T-3 file. The glossy viewed on their flight back from Kandahar looked nothing like this man. The Prophet in that photograph was the man they had seen in concert last night. Had her father been deceived? Could this charlatan have provided her father with a curriculum vitae based entirely on fraud? How had such a massive hoax gone unnoticed by the media? Her volatile temper challenged her to walk out the door, but her ingrained trust in her father demanded substantive answers even if the possibility of this humbug ever ascending to the pulpit of the Spire proved to be DOA.

As she and Ben accepted the invitation to sit down to a meal which had obviously been prepared for their arrival, a young lady stepped out of the kitchen carrying a prosciutto cotto ham roast. Mixed green and herb tossed salads graced the table, served up in individual bowls as part of an elegant five-piece setting she recognized as the Etoiles de la Mer pattern from Versace, similar to a set Beth had received as a wedding present. Buttery rosemary rolls, lemony asparagus, and creamy garlic mashed potatoes completed the festive ensemble.

"Enjoy," said the girl as she set down the platter of ham and disappeared back into the kitchen.

"The idea of the Prophet actually came from your father." DeLoran broke the uncomfortable silence as they began to fill their plates with the tantalizing banquet before them. "The actor you observed at Red Rocks last night has been entertaining crowds for the past eight months. Three other performers have played the part since the original video appeared. Each has been sworn to secrecy and kept their word as required by confidentiality agreements. Make-up artists are responsible for the striking similarities in appearance."

"You're lying." Serenity set down her fork, not certain she could even continue to accept the hospitality of such a fraud. "Father would never have condoned such a hoax, much less been the one to suggest it."

"If you don't believe me, ask Ben here."

"You knew about this? You told me you'd never even seen the Prophet before."

"I had not seen the Prophet. But I have met Michal." Ben focused his attention on the ham and potatoes, bracing himself for what he had known would be Sere's reaction, but unable to prevent the explosion.

"Semantics. The name of Michal DeLoran has been synonymous with the Prophet since "Coming Again" first appeared. This isn't some kind of lip-synced Milli Vanilli. This represents whole-sale fraud. Chicanery. To think that the entire phenomenon of musical evangelism could be based on flimflam. Hoodwinking a gullible populace with smoke and mirrors, song and dance."

Michal finished a bit of his herb tossed salad and calmly took a sip of water to clear his throat. "Miss Edwards. When you went to the concert last night did you go to see the Prophet or did you go to see Michal DeLoran?"

When Serenity just glared at him, he re-directed the question toward Ben who quickly responded.

"I went to see the Prophet."

"Because you already knew it wasn't DeLoran. And you let me think…" She thought about throwing some mashed potatoes. It had been ages since her temper had raged to the place of throwing things, but this situation most certainly rose to that level. Ben had known the glossy lied. He had met Michal DeLoran. Ben had known. She could hardly wrap her mind around that fact without exploding. Besides that, her father had known. What was he trying to do to her?

Ben swallowed a bite of ham before responding. "Sere. I let you think what you wanted to think. As long as you focus on determining the validity of the Prophet as a successor to your father you will not be focusing on the truth. I knew of no better way to challenge your preconceptions than to expose you to both Michal and the Prophet in their own milieu. If a photograph of Michal had been included in the dossier when you were anticipating meeting the Prophet, would you have even come to Denver?"

"Tell me this." Michal speared another piece of ham, his appetite apparently undisturbed by her animosity. "In the dossier your father prepared, did it ever call me Prophet?"

"That's beside the point. It included his picture."

"No, that is the point. I have never under any circumstance claimed to be other than what I am. When I first approached your father with the concept for 'Coming Again' he knew me as a young composer, not as a performer. We both realized that I could never portray on stage what my mind had committed to manuscript paper. In order to bring that dream to completion it would take a talent which I never claimed to possess. Dr. Edwards recognized immediately the potential for reaching young people through a medium which they already embraced. We advertised the production as Michal DeLoran's 'Coming Again,' and people simply assumed that I was like every other rocker out there, determined to control my own destiny by performing my own songs. We didn't even envision the use or popularity of the name Prophet. If I recall correctly, a writer from some British publication came up with that title."

"You should try the asparagus," said Ben. "It's very good."

Serenity glanced down at the food on her plate and cut off the end of a green spear. She strained to keep her bad temper fed even as her palate enjoyed such a wonderful feast. The asparagus was good. "So, if T-3 does not include the Prophet, why should it include Michal DeLoran, or any musician? The InSpire services don't even use any music."

"I wondered about that," said Michal, "especially when your father wrote and asked if I would allow you to come for this interview. Why doesn't he include worship as part of the weekly services? Every other revival has been closely identified with a musician. The name of Moody can hardly be pronounced without its correlative, Moody and Sankey. R. A. Torrey and Charles Alexander. Billy Sunday and Homer B. Rodeheaver. Billy Graham and George Beverly Shea."

"One of the first questions I ever asked Dr. Edwards," said Ben. 'Why no worship? The answer was quite simple. Every one of the revivals you mentioned occurred in the English-speaking world. The InSpire revival has been worldwide. Hymns by Sankey worked spiritual magic in both the United States and Great Britain. Rodeheaver's trombone and gospel choirs mesmerized audiences in both Peoria, Illinois, and New York City, New York. But today Southern Gospel choruses, popular in the Ozarks, sound like hillbilly music to Californians. Contemporary Christian doesn't cut it in Calcutta. Music may be the universal language, but its dialects still resist translation into foreign cultures. Dr. Edwards found it easier to eliminate music altogether than to attempt to satisfy the cultural preferences of one hundred and eighty distinct musical tastes."

The waitress started into the room with a tray of Lamingtons, elegant sponge cakes from Australia, only to be waved away by Michal who realized Serenity still had most of her food left on her plate. "American hymnody has always suffered when translated into other languages. I remember a story from one missionary who thought he translated lyrics about the Holy Spirit only to discover that he was encouraging the nationals to sing the praises of bicycle tires."

"So, what has changed?" Serenity cut her ham into smaller pieces, avoiding eye contact with either of the men. Her anger didn't really need to be directed at them. Her father was the one who had some questions to answer. Why did he send her on this futile quest if he had already vetted the men? What purpose was there in seeing their ministries personally? Especially if Michal DeLoran and the Prophet had separate identities? Why Daniel? Why Billy? None of them made any sense if he wanted the ministry to proceed in the same direction he had been leading. That could only happen under Ben's leadership and he wasn't on the list. "So, what do you gentlemen think has changed? Does my father want InSpire Ministries to become a spiritual MTV? Should worship music totally replace the preaching of the Word?"

Both men started to answer simultaneously. Michal nodded toward Ben to go first. "Your father and I have been considering the future of the ministry since long before he grew ill. His greatest concern has been continuity. Historically, revivals have been notoriously short-lived. Think about the kings of Judah. One would lead a revival, and his son would reverse the trend. The Welsh Revival lasted less than a year. The Great Awakening impacted America for almost two decades, but then disappeared. Your father appreciated the way Daniel expanded the transoceanic impact of the ministry. As for Michal? I think you need to allow him to answer for himself."

Serenity nodded and divided her attention between the musician and the meal. The asparagus really was good.

"My background has not been in rock music. I began to sing in church at age four. My parents entered me in a local talent singing contest at six, and a national piano contest at seven. They paid for lessons from a classical musician. My own choice included studying violin and clarinet without a teacher. I joined the civic orchestra as a violinist at age nine. Growing bored with the music they played, I decided to compose. My first symphony was selected as a competition finalist when I was eleven. I didn't win because the judges discovered my age and were afraid it would embarrass all the other contestants to be beaten by a pre-teen."

This time he allowed the waitress to place the Lamingtons in front of them and remove the empty plates. After serving them, the young lady joined them at the table, taking a seat right next to Michal.

"As I said before, the decision to promote the 'Coming' video came from your father. He loved the idea of a youth component to the revival which had begun to spread through InSpire Ministries. At the same time, he recognized the liabilities of music which Ben just explained. Rather than promote the musical on his program, he made me one of his Freedom Projects. Funding, advertising, contacts in the industry which I certainly did not possess. You know the result."

"Success! Just like Ben's mother's books and the Spirit of the Spire Amusement Park. Believe me, I know all about Freedom Projects. But father has never suggested that we turn the entire ministry into a book publisher or that we build amusement parks all over the world. Why music?"

"You're still thinking only of the Prophet. The vision I discussed with your father involves a complete transformation of the universal church's approach to musical evangelism. No longer would we take American hymns and attempt to foist them on cultures steeped in native rhythms. Instead, talented composers in every musical genre would be challenged to produce worship anthems using indigenous genres. West African afrobeats. Cameroon Bikutsi. Arabian Khaliji. Chinese Folk. Japanese Kayokyoku. Laotian Mor lam. Even German electronic cosmic music. Every form conceivable would be infused with spiritual lyrics to the praise of His glory. My own contribution would include a renaissance of the classics, the composition of arias, overtures, operas, and symphonies recapturing the biblical themes of Mozart, Handel and Verdi."

"Delicious," said Ben, swallowing a bite of sponge cake and acknowledging their server with a nod. "I remember a lyric from a children's musical that said, 'Sing it. You'll never forget it.' The long-term effects of your father's ministry could be extended for generations if the biblical principles he teaches could be enshrined in collective cultural memories through music. Not American music, but indigenous music."

"Sir Oliver's Song," smiled Michal. "Loved that as well."

Serenity lingered over her dessert, allowing herself time to think. She did desire a long-term impact from her father's ministry. Whether she liked it or not, the responsibility for continuity had been dropped into her lap. Was it possible that the best way to facilitate enduring revival lay in the development of universal worship through music? Could the approach Michal envisioned be part of the educational system Daniel had outlined? Between the pleasure to her palate and the pressure on her brain, she almost missed the next comments from her host.

"I already told Dr. Edwards that I will not be the one to succeed him at the Spire. I probably should have introduced you to our hostess earlier. Amelia, our guests today are Serenity Edwards and Benjamin Morris. Serenity and Ben, Amelia is my fiancée. We are planning a September wedding. That disqualifies me for the Spire appointment."

"Congratulations," said Ben. "But I don't see any disqualification there. Timothy Three specifically mentions being the husband of one wife. Seems like you have added a qualification."

Michal placed his left hand over Amelia's right and squeezed lightly. "Oh, but it does. The husband of one wife means that I could never marry Serenity."

# CHAPTER TEN

Serenity could recall only two previous occasions when she had been so completely flummoxed. Michal's announcement was the third.

On Valentine's Day in third grade, Rusty Schumacher had pursued her all over the playground. No other word except pursued could possibly apply. Stalked might have fit if they had been older. The class party still lay in the future. No one had opened the gaily decorated boxes containing home-made or purchased cards. To leave out any individual would have been unthinkable, even though each card contained hearts and smarmy sentiments like Winnie the Pooh's "Love is just a word until someone comes along and gives it meaning." Or the much simpler "Be Mine!" carved on a candy heart.

She had been playing hopscotch with a group of girls when she noticed Rusty cut in line and start jumping from space to space behind her. Turning to chastise him for interfering with their game, she barely avoided his clumsy lunge.

"Go ahead. Kiss her. I dare you." The shout from Glenn Munson alerted her to the seriousness of the situation, and the chase began. She ran fast, but he ran faster. Cheers, jeers and high-pitched screams of disbelief echoed off the brick wall of the school as he planted a sloppy wet one right on her mouth. The teacher allowed her to go home before the party, her Valentine box unopened.

The celebratory dinner marking her entrance into adulthood at eighteen had been planned for weeks. She and Beth had tickets to *Les Miserables* at MTH, Musical Theater Heritage. Reservations in the historic Freight House space at Grunauer's Austrian restaurant had been her father's birthday gift. Guilt had prompted the afternoon visit with her mother: a tea party upgraded to a somewhat festive occasion by two chocolate cupcakes. Leila wore her puffy white blouse, black vest, and red skirt along with her Red Riding Hood cape. She delighted over the cakes, proclaimed the event a perfect picnic in the deep, dark woods, and suddenly gazed at her daughter out of eyes no longer clouded by childish fantasy.

"You're grown up, my dear."

"Yes, mother. I'm eighteen today."

"I've missed you. Where have you been?"

Serenity nearly choked on a bite of cupcake. Where had she been? Where had her mother been? She had failed to recognize her on every visit from the time she was small. Why now, on the cusp of adulthood? Had this latent intelligence always been just below the surface? The need to answer the question grew moot as other, more easily answerable queries followed.

"Where is your father?"

"He'll be here soon. He always comes right after work. You know that, don't you mother?"

"Always. So faithful." Leila gazed around the room. "He takes good care of me. I think he loves me."

"I know he does, mother. We both do. Would you like me to call him?" She caught the eye of the nurse who listened wide-eyed to the unimaginable conversation and tried to get her to understand that a call to Dr. Edwards would be in order.

"No. Don't bother him. I'll see him tonight. Let's finish our meal so we can head on over to grandmother's house."

And that was it. Leila disappeared behind the pale orbs of the girl in the red cape, and Serenity turned away to hide the tears resulting from her one sane conversation with a mother she would never really know. Disappointment. Frustration. Anger. Despair.

Michal DeLoran's abrupt announcement nearly exceeded the magnitude of those two disconcerting reminiscences.

"Marry me?" She choked on the Lamington just as she had done on the cupcake on her eighteenth birthday. "Marry me? Of all the rude, insulting…"

"*Not* marry you," Michal interrupted. "I can't marry you. Which means I can't be your father's successor. That was part of the deal, wasn't it? Marry the heir apparent? That's the whole point of the T-3 Project, is it not? Your father chooses as successor whoever you choose as a spouse."

Serenity rose to her feet, nearly knocking over the chair and looking wildly around for her jacket and purse so she could leave. "How can you denigrate my father in that way? Insinuating that he would offer me up in the marriage market with the ministry as the bride price? How can you even think that I would agree to such an objectionable arrangement? Forget the husband of one wife requirement, you're not even respectful, and certainly not above reproach." Still fuming, she pivoted to include Ben in the tirade as well. "And you. What's your role in all this? Matchmaker? Here to ensure that proper arrangements can be made as soon as the bartered bride agrees with the pre-ordained choice of the establishment? Daniel Ellicott and Michal DeLoran said no, so only Billy Wilson remains. She'll have to choose him."

In the shocked silence which followed, only Amelia seemed to grasp the totality of that which lay beneath the accusations and recriminations.

"She didn't know," she whispered, laying a hand on Michal's knee. "You can't blame this on her. Someone didn't tell her the truth."

"I am truly sorry," said Michal, responding immediately to Amelia's gentle nudge. "When I received the letter requesting this interview and explaining the legal disposition of the commutation of power, I assumed your involvement. I fully expected your response to my announcement to be one of relief. Apparently, your understanding of your father's wishes and the responsibility entrusted to you differs from my presuppositions."

Serenity sat down, her anger subsiding quickly with Amelia's understanding and reception of the obviously sincere apology. "Interviews. Three interviews and a report. That's all he asked of me. He wants the ministry to continue, to grow, to flourish. Even if it were to expand in a totally new direction, he desires that worldwide revival continue. The psalmist said that David served his own generation, and father has done that as well. But the next generation will need a new voice. This has nothing to do with me. Nothing."

Ben had never loved her more than he did at that moment. Passionate loyalty to her father ignited a spirit within her very being which radiated zealous devotion. He longed to see that same spirit kindled in response to his cherishing. He feared he had waited too long. Concealing the truth had saddled him with both a curse and a blessing. Not knowing his name graced the list of successors protected him from the ire just heaped on an unsuspecting Michal DeLoran. Not knowing his name graced the list of potential successors doomed his chances of revealing his heart without the entanglement of Dr. Edwards's impending death, her poignant sense of duty, and skeptical suspicion related to any logical explanation he might offer.

Melvin and Ashley had already filed a flight plan for the journey from Denver International Airport to Chicago's O'Hare, but Serenity insisted those plans be changed. She needed to talk to her father.

# CHAPTER ELEVEN

Beth Guilford whirled onto the tarmac in her red Mazda before Captain Melvin completely shut down the engines on the Gulfstream. When Ashley disarmed the plug door, Serenity dashed down the stairs and the two of them disappeared before Ben collected his luggage.

"You're going to need a ride," observed Ashley. "Someone stirred up the bees in her beehive. Mel and I both have vehicles in the parking lot, but it will take some time to file reports and get this baby into the hanger. If you don't mind waiting, one of us can provide transportation."

"Thanks. But I think I'll call Uber." The trip from Denver with Serenity had been worse than a day of ice-fishing without a shelter in a forty-mile-an-hour wind with nothing biting. He had tried once to encourage a perusal of Billy Wilson's dossier, a suggestion met with obvious hostility, although she did stare long and hard at his glossy. Then again, he could count his blessings that Sere wasn't biting, just seething. If they had been ice-fishing, her heat would have melted the entire lake. He thought about warning Dr. Edwards, but decided the ice was already too thin under his own feet.

A text from his mother triggered a trip across town to her condominium after an Uber ride home to pick up his own vehicle. The Alameda Tower Condominiums had proven to be a good choice for Ricci Morris when she moved to Kansas City. The classical stone façade, observatory-like panoramas from oversized windows, and sumptuous interior finishes, provided both a comfortable home and an ideal workplace. Though pricey, the advance from her latest novel had been more than adequate to cover the cost. Ben made it a practice to stop in at least once a week. The invitation to dinner surprised him only because it meant his mother knew he had returned to town ahead of schedule. But then, she had always seemed to know his whereabouts even during his teenage years.

"My world traveler," she greeted him at the door, pulling him into a warm embrace. "There's someone here I want you to meet."

Typical, thought Ben. She hated surprises and yet managed to surprise him repeatedly. The man who rose from the sofa with an extended hand looked comfortable enough to act as host even though Ben had never seen him before. Slightly taller than him, he noted. Approximately the same age as his mother. Casual chinos and a Timberline sweater harmonized with the short boxed, neatly trimmed beard.

"Tyler." The man shared his name and a grip which proved firm without the pressure some males used to prove their superiority. "Ricci tells me you have just returned from Afghanistan."

"Via Denver," added Ben, returning the handshake. "I'm surprised she knew my whereabouts. I'm supposed to be in Chicago."

Ricci waved her son in the direction of an over-stuffed Manhattan leather armchair and joined Tyler on the sofa. "I knew Serenity would head back as soon as she heard Dr. Edwards had been admitted to the hospital."

"The hospital?"

"She didn't tell you? They kept him after yesterday's treatment, determining his condition too critical to risk the trip home."

The journey from Denver skimmed through his head like a fast-forward movie. Had she received a call when they first boarded the plane? Did the frozen treatment result from her fears rather than from the frustration of the interview with Michal as he had assumed? If she did know, why hadn't she told him? Perhaps a payback for keeping secrets from her?

"That's the first I've heard. How's he doing?"

"Much better today. Tyler and I just came back from there an hour ago. He told us you had cancelled the trip to Chicago for the time being. That's why I sent you the message. He wants to see you, but first you need to eat. I made lasagna."

She called on Tyler to say grace, the first time Ben could ever remember a meal with his mother when he hadn't been asked to do the honors. Apparently, this guest he had come to meet was more than just a good friend. His fear ever since her sensational success as a novelist had been this exact scenario. Some reverse version of the archetypical female gold-digger would appear and convince her to trust him with her fortune. He just hoped it wasn't too late. Playing chaperone for your mother could be like taking the advice of the queen who told Alice, "It takes all the running you can do, to keep in the same place. If you want to get somewhere else, you must run at least twice as fast as that."

Not wanting to appear overtly obvious, Ben waited until the chitchat had continued for several minutes before casually asking the question most on his mind. "So, Tyler, what type of business takes up your time?"

"Oh, he doesn't need to work," said Ricci, fulfilling his worst fears. An out-of-work freeloader. Nothing but trouble.

"I see," said Ben although he didn't see at all. How often did that little two-word phrase twist itself into the exact opposite of its literal meaning?

"He doesn't like to talk about it, but Ty came up with the first Freedom Project, long before mine."

The first Freedom Project. The impetus for the expansion of the Spire into worldwide impact. Ravenel? Of course. The Reversal of Babel. Tyler a gold-digger? Not hardly. His mother's guest was one of the richest men in America.

"I'm sorry. That is, you have no idea what I was thinking. I am thrilled to have met you Mr. Ravenel."

"Tyler, please. And I do have some idea what you might have been thinking. Would you allow me to explain?"

"Over dinner," insisted Ricci. "Lasagna tastes much better when it hasn't had to endure the likes of your interminable lectures."

The casual teasing which characterized their relationship told Ben far more than any potential forthcoming announcement. He wanted to hear Tyler's story, and he wanted to know his intentions toward his mother. Loading his plate with the meaty, cheesy pasta treat prepared just the way he liked—without cottage cheese—he glanced from his mother to Tyler, wondering who would begin.

"I fell in love with her books," Tyler scooped a large serving of lasagna onto his plate and added a couple slices of garlic bread. The incongruity of a space traveler crash landing in a field of talking cornstalks and trying to teach them about God, not knowing if they even possessed souls, somehow appealed to my sense of whimsy. I guess it did for a lot of people, judging from the sales. The more I read, the more I realized that she wasn't writing about cornstalks at all. The theme of every deep space adventure revealed the vastness and awesome majesty of an infinite Creator. Exploring Alpha Centauri and Icarus extended and amplified the exploration of the attributes of God. His power expanded beyond both the now and then, the present and future, beyond the limits of the universe. A God unbound by time, space, or His own material creation. I desired to meet the one who could write such mind-bending theology."

"What he means is that he wanted to meet the *man* who could write such a theological novel." Ricci laid her hand briefly over his. Their eyes spoke volumes before Tyler resumed his story.

"I admit my male chauvinism and repent in dust and ashes, if you admit your name involved a deliberate deception. Ric Morris. What was I to think?"

"May I blame my publisher? Margaret Atwood and Ursula Guin certainly shone brightly in the fantasy firmament. Anne McCaffrey won a Nebula award. But sci/fi still remained the literary domain of the males—Heinlein, Bradbury, Dick, Brooks and Asimov."

"Blame him all you want. I'm just thankful that he facilitated our first meeting." Tyler rubbed his fingers together and pressed them against his chin as if stifling a shiver brought on by the recollection of that one vital event. "There I was in Dr. Edward's office…"

"Tell him why you were there," Ricci grinned, but Tyler allowed no interruptions.

"Later! I had the latest Ric Morris book in my briefcase. When Ernst noticed it, he asked me if I would like to meet the author, just as casually as if he could introduce me to William Shakespeare or Nathaniel Hawthorne. A phone call and several minutes later she walked into the room."

"And you said?"

"Ric?"

"Actually, you said RIC??????"

"I suppose I did." Laying one arm softly over her shoulder he pulled her close and placed a butterfly kiss on her eyelids. Without shifting away, she blinked back tears and smiled into his eyes.

"Now tell him why you were there."

When no reply came, she extricated herself from his embrace while still resting her head on his shoulder. "He doesn't like to talk about himself," she explained to Ben. "Would you like to hear the story of the Reversal of Babel?"

"I would love to."

"Well, you'll have to hear it from me then. The brain of young Tyler Ravenel combined the best of Einstein, Bill Gates, and Steve Jobs in one cerebrum. No greater intelligence had ever breathed the fresh air of mother earth. His mental acumen towered over the landscape like Mount Everest transplanted into the middle of Death Valley."

"Whoa, Nelly! Whoa!"

"Nellie? Nellie Bly? 'Ten Days in a Mad-House' Nellie? You want to tell the story yourself?" Ricci grinned. "Go right ahead." She leaned back in her chair, crossed her arms and dared him to continue.

"I was lucky."

"You were brilliant."

"Someone had already figured out how to use translation technology."

"One language at a time requiring a very expensive download. Very expensive."

"All I did was develop an app that identified the native language of the listener."

"And immediately translated everything the app heard into that native language from that time forward. That's all he did, Ben. Did you hear that? That's all he did."

"Only five languages."

"Plus Ameslan."

Ben had been looking back and forth from one to the other as they played their verbal ping-pong. He grabbed the top of his head in disbelief. "Ameslan? American Sign Language? Really?"

"She exaggerates."

"You understate. Ameslan had to wait for the video version. English, French, German, Spanish and Chinese."

"Dr. Edwards provided the funding, accepting forty-five percent of the shares." Tyler shrugged. "The profits have helped him some over the years."

"When I walked into the office that day, Mr. Genius here had just reported annual profit somewhere in the range of one point two billion dollars."

"Million. One point two million. At least get the facts straight. You're not writing a novel."

"That's all he did, Ben. That's all he did."

Tyler pulled her back into a warm embrace. "We had agreed that every app sold would include a gospel message from Dr. Edwards. If individuals or governments or businesses wanted the technology, they had to accept a direct connection to the Spire. The message had to be heard immediately upon activation of the app."

"And everyone wanted the technology."

"Eventually we expanded to more than one hundred eighty languages. God used that little app to spark a worldwide revival. No amount of profit could ever exceed the joy of playing a small part in a global spiritual awakening. Working with Dr. Edwards had been the greatest joy of my life until I met your mother."

Ben watched the look of mutual admiration which passed between them and decided his skills as a chaperone would not be needed. What he needed was a wedding planner. His mother's next words proved him right.

"Tyler has something else he would like to share with you as well, Ben."

"I know you have always been the most important man in Ricci's life." Tyler began. "I thought it only right to seek your permission, or at least your acceptance, before we announce our plans to get married."

"You don't need my permission. But I will grant it nevertheless. Mom has never been able to play poker, and her face communicates everything I need to know." Holding out his arms he gathered her into a loving embrace as her tears began to flow.

Reaching back toward the sofa, Ricci pulled Tyler into a group hug. "We wanted you to be the first to know. I want you to give me away and we both want you to perform the ceremony. Is such an arrangement even possible?"

"For you, mother, I would even light the candles, unroll the aisle runner, carry the ring on a pillow, and perform special music."

"Not special music," she laughed. "Anything but that."

"All right. No singing. Have you set a date?"

"Tomorrow," said Tyler, pulling her in for a kiss.

"Absolutely not," said Ricci, accepting the kiss but not the ultimatum. "At least allow me to shop for a decent dress."

Tyler turned to Ben and offered his unspoken pledge in a handshake. "I realize your permission may have been unnecessary, but I appreciate it more than you could ever know. There remains another twist to our story which you need to understand. That meeting in Dr. Edward's office was not the first time we were introduced."

Ben's mother wrapped her arms around her fiancé as if to provide physical and moral support for what she knew would come next.

"I knew your mother when she was an undergraduate student at Enderson College. At the risk of sounding like a puny imitation of Darth Vader, I must tell you, Ben. I am your father."

## CHAPTER TWELVE

The sight of her father in a hospital bed, surrounded by bed rails, protective padding, off-set trapeze bars, and a ceiling lift, plus an IV stand, monitor, sterilizers, and electrosurgical units hit her like cold winter wind off the Kansas prairie. How could he have gone from the confident executive behind a power desk to this in just the few days she had been gone?

"We have been keeping him quite sedated because of the pain." The nurse checking the monitor seemed far too young to be entrusted with her father's care. Surely a doctor ought to be in constant attendance. There had to be more they could do for him. Serenity pulled a chair close to the bed and laid her hand gently on top of the covers.

"How's my girl?" Her father's eyes opened gradually as if the eyelids themselves were lifting weights. "Did you have a good trip?"

She grabbed the hand that slid out from under the blankets and held it tight, wishing she could wrap herself in one of the great bear hugs which had always been his way of greeting her.

"I knew you would want a report. Daniel Ellicott enjoys an amazing ministry there in Afghanistan. They love your teaching. We visited only a few of the multitude of house churches he has started, but everywhere we went they were gracious and welcoming. Michal DeLoran? Well, he wasn't quite what I expected."

"I should have warned you that he wasn't the Prophet." Her father laughed weakly. "Wish I could have seen the look on your face. It's always been nearly impossible to surprise you. I wanted you to see for yourself. How about Billy and Ben?"

"We didn't get to Chicago. Not after Lawrence called to tell me you were in the hospital. Why didn't you let me know right away?"

"Lawrence? I told the boy not to bother you. Can't imagine what he was thinking. You didn't need to come. What happens to me is not important. The on-going of the ministry must be our priority."

"That's exactly why I needed to come, father. Apparently there has been a terrible misunderstanding." She hesitated, wondering how she could possibly broach the subject which had come up with Michal when he lay there in pain. But she had to know. It would be impossible to continue with T-3 unless she knew the truth. Who but her father could have given Michal the idea that marriage to her was the requirement for accession to the Spire pulpit?

"Daniel is married to his work," she began. "He has no interest in returning to America, although he assured me of his sincere gratitude for your support. He made it very clear that nothing would please him more than to have InSpire Ministries continue following on the exact path you have been leading. I have no question about his Timothy Three qualifications, but I must agree that he would not fit here in Kansas City."

"He's a good man. One of the best. I wish I could have seen his work first-hand. But I know you are right. He would not adjust well to departure from his chosen calling."

"Michal introduced us to his fiancée, a beautiful young lady by the name of Amelia."

"That's wonderful."

Serenity tried to think of some way to lessen the impact of her accusation, but failed. She had never been able to face her father with anything but the utmost honesty.

"Daniel let us know that he would never leave Afghanistan, and that disqualified him from taking your place. Michal introduced us to Amelia for the same reason."

"I'm not sure I understand. He saw marriage as a disqualification?"

"Not marriage in general, marriage to Amelia. He had been led to believe that he would need to marry me in order to become your successor."

Ernst extended his free hand and manipulated the controls on the hospital bed in order to elevate his head. She could see the pain it caused just to adjust his position but sensed his determination to provide the answers she needed. One part of her wanted to help ease the pain. Another part demanded that he produce the balm which would ease her pain.

"Allow me to begin with a theological discussion and then tell you a story."

Serenity grinned. His father-daughter lectures always began the same way. Explain the scripture. Illustrate the scripture. Apply the scripture.

"At least five different views exist as interpretations of that phrase 'the husband of one wife.' Some theologians claim that the woman in view is the church. A priest must be married to the church, which supports the concept of celibacy. I find that hard to accept when children appear in the context, and the same requirement is made of deacons. Others would argue that it prohibits remarriage of widowers, which does not sync with the rest of scripture where death dissolves the marriage bond. The idea that bachelors, or unmarried men, cannot become pastors has gained acceptance among some. However, Paul does not require 'the husband of *a* wife,' but instead emphasizes the '*one* wife' requirement. If married, he must be faithful to one spouse. That idea of faithfulness prohibits both polygamy, another common interpretation, and divorce, the final of the five views. Paul's concern throughout this passage relates to being above reproach. A pastor must be devoted to one woman. He must love and cherish her in the same way Christ loves His church. Any moral sin of any kind related to marriage must be understood as a disqualification according to Timothy three.'

He reached for the water glass, and she held it so he could take a sip through the straw, then proceeded with his story.

"When I met your mother, she was the talk of the town, the prima donna of Kansas City society. I fell in love with her immediately, not realizing the selfishness of my action. I loved her for what she could bring into our relationship. I looked good when she stood beside me. Her adept conversational skills provided access to inner circles I would never have penetrated on my own. I chose her for my sake, to make myself better. Soon after you were born, everything changed. You know I don't blame you for her medical issues. But she never recovered from the trauma of childbirth. At first, I grew bitter, resentful. It appeared that all my reasons for loving Leila had disappeared. She was no longer admired in society, no longer adept at conversation. I was suddenly ashamed to be seen with her or to even have people know her condition. Oh, they were sympathetic, but a man can only take so much pity."

When she saw him reach for the water on the bedside table, she held it up once again.

"To my shame I actually started to pray that she would die so I could find another who could give me what I needed. I had made a vow for better or worse, but this was worse than worse. My selfishness knew no bounds. Gradually my thinking began to change. I looked at you—small, fragile, and totally dependent on others. You gave nothing and demanded everything, yet I loved you. If I could love a child who had no ability to contribute anything to my life, would it not be possible to love a wife in the same way? I began to value divine love which accepted me when I brought nothing to a spiritual relationship. After many months of grappling with my grudge against God, I managed to offer thanksgiving for a lesson I could not have learned in any other way. Each night after work I would go to her room and look for ways to show her my love. I became Tom Sawyer to her Becky Thatcher, Peter Pan to her Wendy, and Beast to her Beauty. Every time she watched a new video my role changed. I would start each evening as a stranger, and by the time her nurse and I had her settled into bed, our love would be sealed with a kiss—only to start again as a blank slate the next day. I know of no more powerful way to learn the lesson of unconditional love."

Serenity blinked to clear away the tears and kissed his cheek. "I had no idea."

"You didn't need to know. I'm only telling you now because you must understand. I would never force you into a relationship for the sake of my ministry. My greatest desire would be for you to find a husband who accepts you just as you are and spends the rest of his life becoming just what you need. Loving you. Cherishing you. Providing for you in every way. Unconditionally. I would never want someone to love you because of the ministry. And I would never ask you to marry someone you didn't love."

The exertion of sharing his story alerted the nurse who had been watching the monitor from her station. Under her gentle urging Serenity shared a quiet goodbye and made her way back out to the waiting room. She started to phone Beth for a ride when she heard her name being called.

"Miss Edwards, I'm so glad that you received my message." He sat in a straight-backed hospital chair the same way he did behind a desk. Stiff, formal, business-like.

"Hello, Lawrence. I do appreciate it. I never thought he would decline so rapidly."

"All the more reason I need to meet with you about some urgent business. May I offer you a ride back to the Spire?"

"I suppose so. Right now, I'm not sure I could manage a coherent business session, but I do need a ride."

"Nothing more was said as they made their way to the parking lot. Lawrence opened the passenger door on a black Mercedes Coupe and ushered her into the comfortable seat. "Company car," he explained as he slid in behind the wheel. "Wouldn't want you to think I was living *la bella vita* at the ministry's expense."

"My father has always expressed satisfaction with your firm. I apologize if I seem somewhat distracted. It has not been an easy day."

She stared out the window. Uber drivers stopped to collect passengers. Shoppers exited stores bearing multiple brightly colored bags of merchandise. As they passed a park, a boy and his dad played a game of catch. So normal. Everyday life. While her father struggled against the pain of impending death in a hospital bed, life went on undisturbed. She knew the old Chinese parable about the man who couldn't find a household unaffected by sorrow. Everywhere she looked people were probably hurting. But she didn't know their pain. She did know her own.

"When your father asked me to contact you, he expressed a desire that I also explain in greater detail the intention of the T-3 Project, something I thought I had done during our last conversation. Apparently, he received a call from Michal DeLoran after your visit in Denver which concerned him and precipitated his request that you return."

"Michal called him? Father didn't say anything about a call." He had also told her specifically that he had not instructed Lawrence to call her about his condition. Something didn't compute.

Lawrence merged onto The Paseo. "You can't expect him to retain the recall we have all come to expect. I know it is hard to see him this way, but sedation for pain remains the best the physicians can do at the present time. He seemed very disturbed that Michal had assumed that a marriage merger might be part of the Project. I believe I explained the alternative to you in some detail when we met previously."

"You did. But it still came as a shock." She forced herself to shift away from the calming aspect of the movie of normalcy outside the window in order to face the reality of conversation inside the vehicle. "If I do not have a husband when father dies, it will be up to Leila and me to manage the ministry."

"And if she dies, God forbid, it will be up to you. That's what we need to discuss."

Serenity searched for a tissue in her purse and dabbed away the moisture which threatened to destroy the slight amount of makeup applied on the trip from Denver. "Daniel had no interest in leaving Afghanistan. Michal has plans, in addition to his engagement, which don't really fit with the direction father has led the ministry. Billy Wilson still remains a blank page. I can't say that I anticipate a trip to Chicago, but it will be necessary. I do know this. I will not be marrying anyone just so legal requirements of succession can be consummated. Father just made it very clear that such a requirement had never been part of his intention."

"I'm so glad to know he clarified that matter for you. Management of the Spirit of the Spire proves your capacity to assume total control of InSpire Ministries. The potential exists for a future beyond the realm of anything previously effectuated. In order to achieve that latent success, the directors have formulated a plan which I am convinced you would do well to consider. We recommend that you dissolve the corporation."

"Dissolve?"

"Now listen before you react. It would be the best direction for the continuance of your father's ministry. One of your father's deepest concerns has been the vital perpetuity of ministry future. No revival has extended far beyond its progenitor. No successor ever stepped into the shoes of D. L. Moody or Billy Sunday. The Billy Graham Evangelistic Association still exists, but not the massive crusade meetings for which he became famous. You have an opportunity to build on your father's accomplishments rather than see them crumble and fade."

"So instead of buttressing a crumbling structure you propose that we plant dynamite and implode the Spire on itself."

Lawrence exhaled a frustrated sigh. "Statements like that demonstrate your need for legal counsel, Miss Edwards. Please refrain from failing to distinguish between first-hand evidence and what you rush to infer or assume. The Spire would not be demolished, as you so crudely describe. Dissolution of the corporation does not mean cessation of activity. The services from the Spire would not end. Your father's sermons have all been archived and could be re-broadcast for years to come. Someone else could take over that one aspect of the ministry. It would take some time, but another voice could possibly build up the listening audience to at least some semblance of comparison with the amazing success of Dr. Edwards. What the board of directors has suggested encompasses plans far in excess of ongoing preaching. You have been given the opportunity to completely transform the face of worldwide religion."

The excitement in the lawyer's voice struck Serenity as almost zealous. She had never seen him approach any subject with more than an orderly arrangement of legal certitude. Maybe she had misjudged him. There seemed to be a heart beating under the exoskeleton after all. "I assume this alternative meets the approval of my father?"

"Absolutely. In fact, I believe it has been his goal for the T-3 Project from the onset. He knows the men you have been interviewing. All of them have been guests at the Spire. All of them have been the recipients of Freedom grants. He promised you his intention has never been to include you as part of the bargain. So, in the light of the legal requirements of the original plan of succession and the incapacity of your mother, he must have intended for you to retain complete control of the corporation."

"Why, then, a Timothy Three Project at all?"

"To open your eyes to the future. To empower you with a vision of the possible impossible. To enable you to look beyond the immediate to distant vistas. Your father knew that each of those men on the list would encourage a direction for the ministry in line with their personal ambitions. He wanted you to see those limitations in order to provide unlimited inspiration for your imagination. Do you have any idea of the worth of this ministry?"

"Money? You're talking about money?"

"Not just money. Wealth. You know the value of your Spirit of the Spire, I'm sure. Your theme park is one of more than two hundred and fifty Freedom Projects your father funded over the last few years. Each one has enriched the ministry in thanksgiving for his support, even though it has never been required. Donations from profitable sales of the Prophet videos. Income from the staggering worldwide purchases of the Ric Morris novels. The nearly 50 percent ownership of the Reversal of Babel app brings in more than a million dollars every month. The day your father dies you will assume ownership of a corporation worth more than Berkshire, Hathaway, and Apple, Incorporated—combined."

"Do the men—the Timothy Three men—know that?"

"Of course they do. You have to admire a Daniel Ellicott or a Michal DeLoran for turning down that kind of wealth. But I'm convinced that your decision not to consider any of them as partners will accomplish the best for everyone. It's obvious to me that your father trusts you to oversee the expansion of the Spire ministries, with the continued support and advice of our firm. Just think of what could be done. A film industry to rival Hollywood here and Bollywood abroad. A publishing house discovering dozens of Ric Morrises. Support for political candidates who would bring the country back to its spiritual foundations. You could buy the presidency the same way Donald Trump did. An aid association to rid the world of hunger. Spirit of the Spire Theme parks around the globe. Hospitals in Africa conquering AIDS and eradicating Ebola. You have been awarded the possibility of single-handedly guiding the church to its greatest success since the days of the Apostle Paul."

Serenity gazed out the window, realizing they had arrived at the Spire. The sun gleaming off the silver-tinted windows transformed her father's dream into a glowing monument to his foresight and innovation. The soaring tower atop the structure scraped the sky, and yet, the heavens stretched even further beyond. Words from a long-forgotten poem by Edna St. Vincent Millay echoed through her mind.

> The world stands out on either side, no wider than the heart is wide;
> Above the world is stretched the sky—no higher than the soul is high.
> The heart can push the sea and land farther away on either hand;
> The soul can split the sky in two and let the face of God shine through.

Could that really happen? Could her father's legacy become her ambition? Could her soul split the sky in two?

Lawrence exited the Mercedes and played the gentleman, opening the door for his guest. "Please consider carefully what I have shared, Serenity. I know you will want to complete the Timothy quest entrusted to you by your father, but please know that your decision to eliminate yourself from the equation will undoubtedly be the finest decision you have ever made. I am so glad you have decided that you will not be compelled to marry for the sake of the ministry."

She shook her head slightly to clear out the plethora of revelations to which she had just been introduced. "Thank you for the ride, Lawrence. You have certainly given me much to consider." He had done that, although even in her present emotional state she knew his fantastical scheme would never work. The very idea of monetizing the ministry made her nauseous. Social science says, "We have a problem, let's create an agency to look for an answer." But they never find a solution. Why? Because that would mark the demise of the agency. Everyone they hired would be out of work. Her father searched for people who already had solutions and made possible the pursuit of their dreams. Some failed. But when that happened no agency existed to continue the process of incessantly pouring money down a rat hole. It failed and people moved on. Freedom Projects succeeded because a solution had been discovered before funding ever became available. What the lawyer proposed smacked of social science, not Holy Spirit guidance. Whatever happened, she had no intention of dissolving the ministry so money could be invested in agencies. Her father would not approve, no matter what Lawrence Wiley claimed.

"Never forget the trust your father has placed in you." The lawyer handed her a folder similar to those he had given her before the journey to Afghanistan. "Before I leave, please allow me to apologize for an entirely unintentional oversight on my part. After you left for your trip to Kandahar, I realized that one of the dossiers from your father still remained in my briefcase. Here is the file for the fourth man in the T-3 Project, Benjamin Morris."

## Chapter Thirteen

The news that Tyler Ravenel shared with him struck Ben with the force of a silver bullet from the pistol of his childhood hero, the Lone Ranger. He listened in amazement as the two of them shared an account of their brief affair and the fact that his mother left school without ever telling Tyler about her pregnancy. His own invented backstory of a father who didn't love him, who abandoned him and his mother in their time of greatest need, vanished like a shadow in the night.

"My love for your mother in no way justifies my behavior. What we did outside the bonds of marriage was wrong. But I have told her, and I want you to know, that I have spent the past thirty years searching for the only woman I have ever loved."

The joy on the face of his mother provided more than enough evidence to convince Ben that she shared the blessing of the eventual resolution to that search. His own emotions would take a bit longer to reconcile. What would be expected of a son who had never known a father? He had counseled a man who became a Christian later in life and faced the same dilemma concerning a heavenly Father. What did God expect of him when he had grown up without a spiritual father and was now part of the household of God? Did the same rules apply to him as to those who had a relationship with God from early years? Those who had been bounced on His knee from childhood? Would God give him time to learn what it meant to know a Father, or did He expect an immediate transformation from orphan to sonship? Would Tyler expect Ben to become a confidant who willingly sought for and accepted fatherly advice? Could trust develop gradually or would there be a demand like that from well-meaning preachers who expected new believers to simply trust and obey?

There would be time to explore those questions later. Ben stood and extended his hand toward the man who already was, and wanted to become, his father. "Dad," he said. "Welcome to the family."

Rather than shake his hand, Tyler and Ricci rose from the couch and enveloped their son in a warm family group hug over thirty years in the making.

Back in his car, Ben decided another visit would be in order. Serenity would certainly be at the hospital with her father. It would be safe to spend time with Leila Edwards without her daughter's knowledge. He still wasn't sure why he kept his visits with Serenity's mother a secret. It just seemed like the right thing to do. Avoiding any indication that he might be interested in the boss's daughter had been part of his practice since day one at the Spire. He knew it had started as a result of a perceived inferiority. He never felt that he was worthy of Serenity's attention. Later, the feelings had been nurtured by his questions concerning his origins. Over time, the effort to disguise a growing affection for Serenity escalated into a fully developed masquerade. His actions had trapped him like a spider caught in its own web.

"Well, if it isn't Prince Charming." The nurse who admitted him to Leila's apartment greeted him with a smile. His almost daily visits were not a secret to those who cared for Mrs. Edwards. Early on, Leila had tagged him with the Prince Charming name from numerous fairy tales, and the care givers always announced his visits to her in the same way. "She has taken to her bed today," the nurse continued. "We think she has chosen to be the grandmother from Red Riding Hood."

"I'll try not to be the big bad wolf then." Ben walked the length of the sterile room, which seemed to become more like a hospital on each visit, and through the door into the gaily decorated fantasy land where Mrs. Edwards spent her days. Focusing his attention on the bed where she lay dressed in the crocheted night cap of a doting grandmother, he marched across the room and snapped to attention.

"His majesty's woodcutter at your service, ma'am."

Leila giggled in a definitely un-grandmotherly voice. "You can't fool me, Prince Charming. Thank you for coming. Have you met my granddaughter, Little Red Riding Hood?"

Ben spun around to see the very person he had been trying to avoid sitting at the table on the other side of the room. Spread out in front of her, the contents of a familiar file occupied her complete attention. She didn't look up even when her mother introduced her. Ben sat down on the other side of the table and picked up the 8x10 glossy of himself.

"Hello Sere." When she didn't respond, he continued. "So, you know?"

"Now I know. You knew all along."

"I did. And I thought you knew."

"So, it's my fault."

He knew immediately what direction she wanted the conversation to follow. She wanted to go "Into the Woods." One of the games they had often played under the guise of friendly bantering involved using literature and lyrics to frame their conversations. It helped maintain distance by means of speaking someone else's words. Today, however, it didn't seem to be friendly.

"No, I should have said something on the way to Kandahar."

"But you didn't."

"I didn't. So, it's my fault. How is your father?"

"Weak. He says I don't have to marry any of you."

"You don't. Not even if we ask."

"But you let me think so."

"I've never told you what to think. I know better than that."

"So, it's my fault. Why didn't you?"

"Didn't I what?"

"Tell me."

"Fear. Uncertainty. Not knowing the right words to say. Cowardice? I know I should have, Sere. It's entirely my fault."

"I trusted you."

"And I betrayed that trust."

"When did you know?'

"From the beginning."

"The beginning of the Plan? When you and father decided to gamble with my future?"

"Long before that."

She almost looked at him when he said that. Her eyes narrowed as she forced herself to maintain avoidance. "Are we talking about the same thing?"

"Probably not. It's my fault. History has changed."

"You told me history couldn't change. That was your ultimate objection to my plans for the theme park. Re-writing history, you called it. The Descent into Hades roller coaster rewrote history by suggesting people could go to hell and return. They wanted to go again because they had survived. Survival produced false hope. Have you changed your mind?"

"Only if past history proves false."

"So, if historical records have lied, we can change the future?"

"Exactly."

"You want to change the future?"

"Nothing would please me more."

"So, why don't you?"

"Change the future?"

"No, why don't you ask?"

"You aren't ready." He knew she wouldn't accept a touch. Instead he tried to force eye contact and failed. "What if I did ask?"

She wanted to look at him. His eyes would reveal the truth. A truth she still believed impossible. "You're right. I'm not ready."

"Besides, it can't be part of the Plan."

"Father's Plan?"

"You don't deserve that pressure. It can't be your father's choice."

"So, you would have asked? Before the Plan?"

"I've wanted to since the day we met."

"So, it's my fault."

"Not at all. I wasn't ready either. It's my fault."

"And now?"

Before he could answer, Leila called from her bed. "I've been wanting the two of you to meet. Now that you've chased away that big bad wolf, I feel so much better. Did you bring me a picnic lunch?"

Serenity carried a small box of chocolates over to her mother and placed one into her hand. "These are the pink nougats that you like, mother."

"And you carried them all the way through the woods just for me. What a loving granddaughter."

She patted her mother's hand and returned to the table, determined not to lose her composure by making eye contact. How could he claim to have been interested in her all these years? How could the succession plan have changed history? Perhaps the same way it had for her. He wasn't about to be forced into a relationship because of her father any more than she.

They certainly agreed on that, but it still hurt. She pulled a blank sheet of paper out of the file and picked up her ballpoint pen.

"Are you ready for your T-3 interview, Dr. Morris?"

"This is not the time or the place, Sere."

For the first time since he entered the room, she forced herself to look at him. The hurt which resulted from his sudden declaration of interest after so many years of disregard boiled over.

"And when will that be? After Billy Wilson turns me down and you're the only candidate left standing? When father dies, and my remaining choices pivot between marrying someone who can't even bring himself to show any interest in me and dissolving the ministry? Do you think I'll be more ready then? The nurses tell me you've been coming to see my mother in the guise of Prince Charming for years. The same years during which you have treated me like an ugly stepsister. Don't think I haven't noticed how you avoid me. Father must have really twisted your arm to force you to travel with me. Or maybe he just offered you the opportunity in order to enable your best effort toward foisting me off on one of the other candidates."

He started to stand. His hope had been winning her favor when the prize of the ministry was not in play. Now that hope lay shredded at their feet. Just when his heritage made pursuit possible, circumstances destroyed any prospect of success. He glanced at the bed where Leila lay back in contentment on the pillow. "Serenity, please. Think of your mother."

"She can't hear us. She thinks you're courting." She made the word sound like a curse.

"I wish I could."

"Now you tell me."

"It's my fault. I had my reasons."

"The Timothy Project?"

"Not at all. I thought you knew I was on the list. When we left for Afghanistan and my file wasn't in sight, I figured you had already eliminated me."

"I just received it today from Lawrence."

"Lawrence?"

"The law firm—Burnley, Wiley, and Associates."

"He kept it from you?"

"A simple mistake."

"So, it's his fault?"

"Not if you already knew."

Ben resumed his seat, resigned to the prospect of cross-examination. "So, what do you need to know?"

"The same questions posed to Daniel and Michal. What would you do with the ministry?"

"Nothing."

"Nothing? You're turning it down just like they did?"

"That's not what I said."

"You said, 'nothing.'"

"I would do nothing, change nothing. What your father has done with InSpire Ministries resulted in a worldwide revival. Why would I change that? The attention of the media for years has focused on the Freedom Projects. Every newscast, every article, and the many unauthorized biographies talk about the success of your father's monetary investments. To them the ministry exists for the purpose of discovering creative individuals and funding them so they will in turn support the Spire. Ernst Edwards discovers the Prophet. Edwards provides seed money for a cancer cure. "Messiah Quest" video-game popularity stems from Edwards's endorsement. The Spirit of the Spire Theme Park, Ric Morris novels. The list seems endless. But they all missed the point. The success of InSpire Ministries does not come from the actions of those who have been affected by your father. The success of InSpire Ministries comes from the minds and hearts of those who have been affected by his words. In order to do something for God, you have to be something for God. In order to be something for God, you need the indwelling of the Spirit of God who uses God's revelation of Himself to transform lives. The one aspect of your father's ministry which must not be changed is the faithful, daily communication of the truth of God's word. Only that truth will set individuals free to please God and accomplish projects for His glory."

He was right. She knew he was right. His words mirrored exactly what her father desired. He had invested himself into Benjamin Morris for this very reason. Her father had chosen a successor for her, knowing exactly what her own choice would be. The T-3 Project had been instituted with one purpose in mind. She could choose Benjamin Morris as her father's successor and nothing in the ministry would change. But she couldn't choose him for herself unless he chose her, even if she did love him. And she did love him. As long as his name had not been on the list, she could reason that the fault lay in him. She could conclude that her father knew something no one else knew. Something which disqualified him in accordance with

Timothy Three. History had changed when the lawyer handed her that file. Now the fault lay in her. She could believe that Dr. Benjamin Morris loved the ministry. But she couldn't believe that Ben Morris loved her. Not after years of silence. History couldn't change that quickly. She sat with her head down, staring at the 8x10 glossy, silent as a sphinx, until he finally crossed the room, kissed her mother on the cheek and walked out of her life.

## CHAPTER FOURTEEN

"It's halftime here at Ambassador Field in Chicago." The familiar voice of longtime announcer Teddy Knopfel rang out over the packed stadium. "What a game! Tied at fourteen. The Chicago Football Team and the Dallas Football Team entered this game undefeated. But that will change today."

Television cameras swept the field as Knopfel brought a national audience up to date on the score Then they focused on a solitary figure standing in the middle of the field. He looked like a wide receiver, two hundred and thirty pounds arranged on a lanky frame, spelling trouble for any defender who attempted an open field tackle. He wore the uniform of neither football team. Instead, as the cameras zoomed in for a closeup, viewers saw a bright blue shirt, red vest, and white blazer. Billy Wilson stood ready for action.

"A tied game. An undefeated season in the balance." The commentator continued to talk as the cameras set the stage. "Yet here at halftime, no one in this magnificent stadium, built on the strength of the Chicago team's many trips to the Superbowl, is thinking of brats and nachos. Instead, their minds have turned to religion. You heard me right. Religion. For the next five minutes, thousands here in Chicago and worldwide will listen as the most dramatic young evangelist ever to hit the American scene illuminates our minds about life, death, and the future."

Serenity watched in anticipation as the face of Billy Wilson appeared on the one hundred and sixty-foot-wide jumbotrons at either end of the stadium. She had read his dossier on her flight north. Professional sports hit rock bottom because of drug abuse right after Billy had been drafted by the Chicago team in the first round. Owners had tried treatment programs, suspensions, fines, and even a psychic. Madame Sylvestia had invaded the minds of addicts, trying to convince their subconscious of the harmfulness of opiates. Nothing worked. Not for football. Not for soccer. Not for the Olympics. Then athletes had started dying. A German skating champion. An NCAA all-star. Brazil's latest soccer phenom. Multiple deaths. Instant. Shocking. The drug habits of professional sports figures, funded by their colossal salaries, became as well-known as ERAs, quarterback sacks, and golden boot awards.

Billy's spiritual decision had not been dramatic. He had slipped away after a game in Kansas City, taken a seat in the back row of the Spire, and listened as Dr. Edwards explained a paragraph from the writings of St. Paul in the book of First Corinthians. The announcement of his decision, by contrast, proved to be extremely dramatic. A sports reporter, searching for a new angle to spice up his Superbowl article, heard a rumor about Billy's escape from drugs. Suddenly, all the networks began scrambling for interviews. Billy never hesitated to credit his conversion with saving him from death by personal lethal injection, a far too common phenomenon that reporters insisted on describing as accidental overdose. "The only possible answer to the drug problem," became his tagline.

The owner of the Chicago Football Team had grown livid. The league had survived the decision to eliminate all team names in order to prevent possible offense. They had regained some of the viewers lost to the boycott when they refused to agree to the Women's Lives Matter Movement, demanding they require every team to hire a female place kicker. They had even survived the stadium name change from Soldier Field to Ambassador Field, made to please the anti-military crowd. But drugs remained a different story. Every player had signed a non-disclosure statement promising not to discuss drug use in any interview. In a desperate attempt to calm his boss down, an assistant coach joked that maybe they should capitalize on Wilson's experience in order to bolster sagging attendance. To Billy's amazement, a press conference announcement by the owner indicated that Billy Wilson would be sharing his secret of how to escape from drug addiction with the entire Chicago Football Team at their next practice, which happened to be that afternoon.

Several players stayed after the meeting to talk with him about their own addictions. He shared the InSpire app with them and promised to keep their confidence. But a reporter scurried to his editor with the breaking news that Billy had given an invitation, and half the team had responded.

Suddenly tickets for the Superbowl, which car dealers had been giving away as promotional incentives for simply taking a test drive, couldn't be purchased at any price. Other club owners, anxious to profit from the publicity windfall, stumbled over each other trying to line Billy up for opportunities to share his secret with their players.

Amazing as it seemed to those in the sports world, Billy's secret worked. By the next season almost every professional football player had the InSpire app on his cell phone. Drug abuse declined. The invitations poured in from hockey leagues, basketball leagues, and European soccer teams. When the Olympic Committee invited Billy to the opening ceremony of the upcoming games, he decided to seek his release from the Chicago Football Team in order to enter fulltime evangelism. They agreed on the condition that he would appear at halftime of every home game to share his story with the crowd. Every game since that time had been a sellout. Billy had shown the world of sports professionals that you could be a winner without artificial aids. Even more important had been the sense of relief that no one had to keep up with the latest narcotic kick in order to gain acceptance.

"May I have five minutes of your valuable time?" The phase had become the trademark of his halftime presentations. Billy Wilson's mic went live, and the full house grew silent.

"Many years ago, an athlete by the name of Paul made an audacious claim, even putting it into print. 'I can do all things,' he said. All things? Say that to Muhammad Ali and hear him shout, 'I'll sting you like a bee in the ring.' Let Michael Jordan hear you say that and find yourself challenged to a slam dunk competition. Lionel Messi would say, 'meet me on the pitch.' Usain Bolt would simply laugh and leave Paul in the dust. In my former life I would have said, 'Paul, what kind of pixie dust are you on?'"

Billy stood alone on the fifty-yard line. No gaudily dressed performers provided back up. The hundreds of dancing volunteers so often associated with halftime did not appear. Stark white stadium lighting did not yield its place to the exotic pink, purple, orange, and blue shades of stage radiance. No Bible. No notes. No pulpit.

"All things, Paul? What about career-ending concussions? What about failure to attain preseason goals? Have you ever faced betrayal and rejection? Do you know what it is to be demeaned because of your skin color? How could he possibly walk into a locker room of today and make such a claim. 'I can do all things.'"

Serenity glanced around at the people near her in the stands. Popcorn and soda sales had ceased. No one seemed to be checking their phones for the scores of other games around the league. The teams on the sidelines sat quietly on their benches, waiting for Billy to finish before heading into the tunnel. Even the color commentators, who always had a statistic to contribute to the action, remained silent.

"Every athlete knows there are three elements which must be present to have a winning team. Confidence. You have to believe you can win. How often have you heard a broadcaster say, 'The momentum has changed, they have their confidence back?' Boldness. Ya'all been accused of being cocky? You know you'll never win unless you have a passion for success. Babe Ruth was known as the king of strikeouts. Led the American League in that record five years straight. But he was also known as the home run king. He had boldness. The third quality needed is endurance. Sticking with it to the end. Never giving up. The Miracle on Ice. The Evil Empire versus the Curse of the Bambino. Paul had all three of those necessary elements for success. But his confidence, boldness, and endurance were not in himself. We must not let his statement echo like a truncated sound bite. The second phrase carries even more impact than the first. 'I can do all things,' he said, 'through Christ.' No pride here. No machismo. No presumption. No reason to go head-to-head with Messi, Jordan, or Ali. Paul chose to be confident, not in himself, but in Christ. To Paul, he himself was nothing. Christ was all. After a decimal point, every zero makes number one worth less. Before a decimal point every zero makes number one greater. Don't put your nothingness ahead of Christ."

Billy stood almost completely still at midfield. His only action involved turning slowly to face a different part of the stadium. All the power came from the impact of his words.

"Boldness—in Christ. Most of us read Paul's words the way we read a text message, through our own presuppositions. I can do some things by myself, but in all other things I need help from the Lord. I need his help for spiritual matters, but winning games is up to me. For that I need drugs. I need Him when I end up in the hospital for concussion protocol, but otherwise, forget about it. Paul knew that if he was doing anything without Christ it wasn't being done in the best way. Endurance—through Christ. Every sporting event has a time limit, even baseball. No one wins until the fat lady sings, according to sportscaster Dan Cook. Christ doesn't change the length of the game, he changes those of us who play the game. Paul didn't say Christ would change the distance from third to home or blind the goalkeeper to an incoming penalty kick. He doesn't change what happens to me, instead he strengthens me so I can endure. He doesn't make me strong through drugs or through success, through religion or even through love. He becomes my strength, and I endure because He never fails. He never fails."

Five minutes and it was over. No invitation. No prayer. Billy left the field. The teams scurried off to their dressing rooms for pep talks from coaches. Hawkers resumed the sale of hot dogs, pretzels, and beer. Fans stretched. Kiss cams roamed the crowd. Announcers brought everyone up to date on the scores of other games. Outwardly nothing had changed. But more than one person in the stadium looked at the half page ad InSpire Ministries had purchased in the program and added the Reversal of Babel app to their cell phone. He had planted. Others would water. God would bring the increase.

# CHAPTER FIFTEEN

Serenity slipped from her seat after the kickoff for the second half. The Wilson Rally bus idled on Museum Campus Drive, ready for the trip to Terre Haute, Indiana, where 75,000 people were expected for an evening rally. The red, white, and blue exterior of the Monaco Dynasty 45P tour bus sported a larger than life size image of Wilson catching a game-winning pass in the Superbowl.

"Miss Edwards?" A broad-shouldered male specimen, worthy of inclusion on any defensive line in the NFL, offered his muscular aid as she made her way into the most luxurious recreational vehicle she had ever seen. The decorating theme screamed sports, while the amenities proclaimed value. Dark oak cabinetry lined the walls over marble countertops. Porcelain tile floors reflected the gleam of recessed LED lighting. A massive TV screen dominated the space, tuned to the still ongoing game at Ambassador field. Overhead, a globe-shaped skylight revealed the blue of a perfect fall day. Overwhelmed by the elegance of the RV, she gave only a glance at the men seated at the far end of the room, watching the game. Before she could absorb the entire scene, Billy entered from what had to be the master bedroom.

"Serenity. I see you have already met Deke, the meanest tackle ever to play for Philadelphia. The other member of my first string is this bruiser on the couch, my driver and manager Phil Matthews, former fullback for Jacksonville. And of course, you already know Ben. Deke, why don't you rustle up some Monte Cristos? I could eat a whale."

Phil and Ben stood while Billy escorted her to the other leg of the leather-covered couch, and Deke made his way to the state-of-the-art kitchen. With the push of a button, a small table rose up from the floor, transforming the seating area and footstool into an opulent Roman triclinium with seating for three. The TV screen receded into the wall, replaced by a basketball hoop which Phil promptly put to good use, swishing in a goal from where he sat. Serenity ducked. Billy grabbed the ball and threw it hard toward the front of the bus.

"Take your ball with you, and let's get on the road."

Phil chased the ball and tossed in another basket as if he were on the free throw line.

"Don't worry. We'll get you to Terre Haute in good time." The 600HP diesel engine had already been idling, and Phil quickly maneuvered the bus onto Museum Campus Drive and in the direction of Indiana.

With just the three of them seated around the table, Serenity could no longer ignore the man she thought she had left behind in Kansas City. Melvin and Ashley hadn't heard from him before she boarded the Gulfstream, and neither had she.

"I hadn't realized you would be at the game, Ben." The last thing she wanted was for Billy to sense tension between them. Neither Daniel nor Michal had been surprised that they had conducted the T-3 interviews together. Billy had undoubtedly received the same notice from her father as the others and expected the same.

"Actually, I didn't make it. Deke and Phil and I watched the halftime show here on the big screen."

Billy grabbed the nerf basketball from where it had fallen and tossed it to Deke, who made an underhanded attempt at a goal and missed completely. "I thought it went well," he said. "At least the peanut peddlers kept quiet. It's hard to compete with popcorn and cotton candy."

"I was amazed that the teams stayed on the sidelines until you finished." Serenity watched as the two of them continued their impromptu basketball battle, while at the same time Deke handled the griddle like an old pro.

"Old friends, all of them. Almost every man on the gridiron any given game day has a best friend on the opposite team. I played ball with almost as many of the Dallas guys as those who are now part of Chicago."

"Friendship's part of it." Deke dropped a sandwich soaked with batter onto the hot griddle with one hand while catching a pass from Billy with the other. "The coaches have realized what the owners still hate to admit. Billy's good for the guys. His talks have changed lives, including mine."

"The way you worked sports metaphors into that verse from Paul certainly resonated with the crowd." Ben jerked as the basketball landed in his lap and stared at it as if he had no idea what he was seeing.

"Sports provides a natural connection to religion." Billy grabbed five plates out of the oak cupboards and stacked them close to Deke's workplace. "In many ways football and other sporting events have become worldwide religions. The largest gathering spots in the nation have been built for college football teams. Some of the high school stadiums in Texas even rival those college venues. Crowds at soccer games in England on any given Sunday far outdistance the number of parishioners in all the churches and synagogues. That made those very stadiums the obvious place to share my story." Deke plopped the first sandwich onto the top plate, and Billy carried it forward to where Phil guided the Wilson Rally bus through Chicago traffic.

"Basketball not your game Ben?" Deke reversed the direction of the Monte Cristos still on the griddle and then slid out a foosball table hidden in one of the drawers next to the stove. "The four of us can play while these suckers cook."

Ben shook his head as Billy re-appeared from the front. "Is there anything you don't have in here, Wilson?"

"Well, there's not enough room for cricket, but the table in front of you reverses into miniature ping-pong, and a putting green slides out from under the couch."

"A net can be dropped down from the ceiling just behind Phil's head as a soccer goal. We try not to play while he's driving. He's so competitive he thinks he can goalie and chauffer at the same time." Deke piled a sandwich onto each of the remaining plates, placed them on the triclinium table, and joined the others on the couches. With seating designed for three, Serenity found herself scrunched between Deke and Ben, feeling like a tabby cat caught between two huge mastiffs. Deke and Billy immediate stuck their thumbs up in the air, and she proudly caught on before Ben, leaving him to say grace.

"Let me know if you want seconds. Phil and Billy and I seldom go with less than three. Then we can show you the best game of all—Madden NFL. You can even choose Billy here for your team, although heaven knows he's slowed down too much to actually compete anymore." Deke jumped up to prepare more eats, at the same time punching the button that re-opened the widescreen.

"Decimating your Philadelphia failures online will have to wait, Deke. Serenity and Ben have an interview to conduct." Billy closed the television monitor and carried another sandwich forward to Phil.

"So, you're going to convince him to quit the road trips? Seems a shame when the schedule is so full."

Serenity fielded the question with her mouth full of ham, turkey and cheese, swallowing hard so she could form a coherent reply. "I don't plan to convince him of anything, Deke. Father just asked me to speak to several different individuals in order to help him choose a successor."

"Right. Ellicott over in Kandahar, the Prophet, Ben here, and Billy. Seems to me like anyone of them would do him proud. Hard shoes to fill, though. That study through Galatians rearranged my entire world view. How's he doing, anyway?"

"The doctor wouldn't release him from the hospital after his last checkup. I don't know how much longer he'll be with us."

"Sorry to hear that." Billy rejoined them after resupplying his plate from Deke's griddle. "Ready for another, Ben?"

"They are great. But I think one will do. Thanks. I obviously don't run off as much energy as the three of you, sitting behind a desk all day."

"None of us are in the shape we once were," said Billy.

"Speak for yourself, tubby." Deke joined them on the couch, two Monte Cristos piled on his plate. "I can still take you down any day of the week."

"Check the win-loss record. That's all I can say."

Serenity swallowed the final bite of her meal and shook her head when Deke tried to slide a sandwich from his plate onto hers. "What does your schedule look like, Billy?"

"Phil would be the best one to answer that, since he does all my planning. But glance over there at the wall. Looks like a full season."

The large chart hanging on the end of the kitchen cupboard featured a background of Billy in uniform. Superimposed over his larger than life figure, a six month calendar revealed locations and times of meetings on almost every square. Halftime shows. Youth rallies. Sunday services. Late-night TV, and early morning radio interviews. A visit to the White House.

"How would you handle all of that if you were to succeed my father?"

"I've wondered that myself, Serenity. It was my first question when I fielded Dr. Edwards's phone call. But he was more interested in the direction I thought the ministry should take than he was in schedules. Let me tell you what I shared with him. I see myself as a recruiter. Athletes listen to my story and sign a contract with God, recognizing the privilege of serving on his team. A recruiter is always on the move. He doesn't attend practices and very seldom gets to sit in the stands and watch a game. There is always one more school to visit, one more player to interview, one more rookie to persuade. I have about twelve five-minute challenges like the one you heard today and maybe eight full-length sermons, most of which are variations of my personal spiritual journey. But that's all I need, because my audience always changes. That wouldn't work if I replaced your father. My approach as a recruiter needs to be supplemented by someone like him. I call your father the coach, the trainer. He takes the rookies and teaches them the game book. My vision for the Spire would be to clone your Dad and produce hundreds of recruiters. One for every football team in the nation, from high school through the pros. One for every soccer team in Europe and South America. One for every cricket team in India. One for every basketball team in the Philippines where they love b-ball even more than here, if possible. InSpire would continue as our coach to provide spiritual training for every athlete recruited for God's team."

"Isn't that what Dr. Edwards and Ben are already doing?" Deke gathered up the tableware and deposited everything into a full-size dishwasher. "Seems to me that both the recruiting and the coaching are pretty important. They taught me in philosophy class." He stopped and grinned. "Don't look so amazed. Athletes can handle philosophy. I learned that the two most important words in the history of mankind are the words 'I think.' The greatest evidence of divine creation remains the mind of man. Evolution tries to explain physical changes, but it can't even begin to explain intelligence. Lions attack and kill but they don't raise money and undertake campaigns trying to convince the rest of the pride that the killer should now become king or president. As I see it, the success of the Spire results from the dissemination of the truth. I'd sure hate to see Billy confined to a desk. He'd soon be as flabby as Ben." Grabbing up the basketball he threw it in Ben's direction, challenging him to try for a basket. "Must take hours to prepare what he and your father share week after week."

"Thanks for the endorsement, Deke." Ben tossed the nerf ball into the air and surprised them all by swishing it through the net.

Serenity knew Deke was right, but this wasn't about Ben. At least she didn't want it to be about him. There was obviously no place for her in the picture if he took over the ministry. He had made that absolutely clear. No one was going to make the choice of a husband for her. Not her father. Not her mother. And certainly not Deke Birch. They all kept telling her she had freedom to choose, and then tried to punch the ball out of her arms to make her fumble. What she wanted to do was get in their faces like a home plate umpire and eject them from the game. Instead she turned to Billy and continued the interview.

"So, would you be willing to move to Kansas City and assume the responsibility of leading the entire InSpire organization?"

"Where I live doesn't really matter." He flipped over the now empty table to reveal the miniature table tennis game and tossed a paddle to Deke. "I basically live here in the RV. Dr. Edwards allows me to borrow the Gulfstream when I travel abroad, so that wouldn't change. If I were in charge, I would continue to travel, and hire Ben here to do the weekly broadcasts. From what I have heard he comes about as close to resembling a clone of your father as possible.'

As Deke and Billy engaged in a rapid-fire version of ping-pong on the tiny table, Serenity tried to keep herself from screaming. Just quit the games and get serious, she wanted to yell at them. Don't keep telling me how wonderful Ben would be in my father's place. I already know that. It's not going to happen. In frustration she blurted out the only question she could think of that would bring the table tennis contest to a halt and convince them all to grow up.

"What would you say if the only way to gain legal control of the ministry was to marry the boss's daughter?"

Deke slammed the ball down hard, and Billy didn't even try to return it. He turned to face Serenity, taking both of her hands in his. "Miss Edwards, if that was a proposal, I accept. A man would be out of his mind to refuse such an invitation. I have heard many speak of your classic beauty, comparing you to Grace Kelly, Jackie Onassis, and even Nefertiti, the most exquisite face ever to be carved in marble. But not one of those gorgeous women can begin to compete with your elegance. Marrying you would be like winning the Superbowl, World Cup, and Olympics all in the same year."

"It's settled then. When can you come to Kansas City so we can conclude this T-3 Project with my father once and for all?"

# Chapter Sixteen

A call to Melvin and Ashley assured a ride for Serenity back to Kansas City from the airport in Terre Haute. Phil dropped her off at Departures, and Ben said nothing about how he would get home. At that point she told herself she didn't care. Ashley left the cockpit and joined her on the short trip, full of news about her latest checkup and the impending arrival of their firstborn. Thankfully, there were no questions about the progress of the T-3 Project. That changed as soon as Beth picked her up at the airport.

"Something is different, Sere. I can see it in your eyes. Does he fill out a suit jacket as powerfully as he used to do those uniforms? There's nothing like a muscled powerhouse in a football jersey to make a girl's heart flutter. Just don't tell Tony I said that."

"Right. As if you wouldn't say the same to his face. So, here's the scoop before you hyperventilate. Billy Wilson stands six-four, looks like a Hollywood star, fills out an XXL sweatshirt with little room to spare, lives in a chic motor home surrounded by other gridiron giants, and is coming here to ask for my hand in marriage as soon as he has a break in his supercharged schedule."

Beth hit the brakes to avoid a collision with a pickup truck whose driver had suddenly decided to cut her off. "He's what?"

"Coming here to..."

"Shut your mouth. I heard all that. You can't just dump a message like that as if it were a Facebook post. What am I supposed to say? Couldn't you at least include some emoticons? A happy face or two? The last I knew you were determined not to accept any proposal from this list your father compiled. Billy Wilson? What about Ben? Was he there? Don't tell me you did this right in front of him. What were you thinking, girl?"

Serenity slumped down in her seat. "I'm not sure I was thinking. I asked him what he would do if I were part of the package, and before I knew it his cohorts had a visit to the Spire on his schedule, right after a stop at the White House. He's perfect for the ministry, Beth. Dynamic, charismatic, eloquent, attractive. You should have seen the way he gripped the attention of that entire crowd in Ambassador Stadium."

"But is he perfect for you?"

Serenity didn't answer. Instead she pulled herself upright, straightened her shoulders, and stared at the lights emanating from the Spirit of the Spire which could just be seen in the distance. "Take me to the park, Beth. I need to check something out."

The forty-acre amusement park accepted visitors as early as 9:00 a.m., but the well-maintained grounds transformed into a magical space after dark. Blue streams of light marked the rails and passing cars of the Exodus from Egypt monorail system which circled the entire complex. The eight quadrants all featured variegated illumination: red, orange, yellow, green, blue, indigo, and violet creating a Noahic rainbow, with white marking the main entrance. Serenity rushed Beth past the ticket booth and inserted her passkey in an unmarked side entrance.

"Hurry! The next round of Religious Wars is about to begin."

The illuminated sign on the front of the building flashed a list of twenty-four "War experiences." David and Goliath. Puritan Witch Trials. The Monkey Trial. The Coliseum. Crusades. The one flashing red and counting down to departure in one minute read, "Spanish Conquistadors versus Montezuma and the god Huzilophochtli."

"Don't let anyone tear your heart out and eat it," Serenity called over her shoulder to Beth as the attendant checked their seatbelts and activated the machinery which plunged them into the middle of an ongoing battle. Montezuma marched out from his castle surrounded by two hundred warriors, barefoot and dressed in a variety of elaborate costumes. Only the ruler wore sandals, indicative of his status as a god. Beth ducked as a myriad of rocks, arrows and spears targeted them, released from the hands of his warriors. In contrast, Serenity stood and returned fire, using a crossbow and shooting numerous bolts in the direction of their attackers.

"How do you do it?" Beth raised her head over the edge of the seat, realizing that the weapons of the attacking army never reached their destination, while the arrows released from Serenity's crossbow seldom failed to accomplish their mission.

"Computer enhanced video projection. Virtual reality. You feel like the battle surrounds you, but the paying passenger always survives. Anything else wouldn't be good for repeat customers. The number up in the right-hand corner keeps track of your kills. My record is sixty- four Aztecs. The average is thirty-seven."

Beth blinked as they emerged into the light, the two-and-a-half-minute ride complete.

"Now, here's the key question. Would you go again?"

"In a New York minute. But this time I want one of those arrow-shooting gun things."

"Crossbows. All right. Exhibit one. On to number two."

For over two hours Serenity charged through the park, never having to stand in line—one of the perks of being the owner. Beth came close to losing her lunch on the Ascension Helicopter, the open-air cage hanging from its belly advertised as "the closest thing to heaven this side of the rapture." They donned lightweight, but authentic looking chain mail as recruits in the crusader army of Richard the Lion-hearted and Frederick Barbarossa. The two of them served as part of the jury in Dayton, Tennessee, listening to Clarence Darrow and William Jennings Bryan engage in a raging debate over evolution before voting to declare John Scopes guilty. At the end of every encounter, Serenity asked the same question.

"Would you like to go again?"

Every time Beth answered with an enthusiastic "Yes," which caused her companion to carry her off in a different direction. Eventually they arrived at the final destination—the Descent into Hades.

Every theme park in the world boasted the merits of their roller coasters—higher, steeper, faster. The Spirit of the Spire added a new element—deeper. The click-clack of the slow-motion ascent mirrored the previous encounters of experienced coaster riders. But the end of the ninety-foot plunge from the top did not stop when they reached the ground. The rest of the ride continued underground with all the twists, turns, drops, and spirals of a Takabisha in Japan or Kingda Ka in New Jersey. The difference lay in the light, or the lack thereof. Macabre and nightmarish scenes from Hieronymus Bosch illuminated the walls just before sharp turns rescued the riders from joining his depictions of hell. Gustave Doré's "Fall of the Rebel Angels" appeared in a holographic image through which the train cars raced. Garish depictions by Peter Paul Rubens and Albrecht Durer brought the horror of eternal damnation into brilliant relief amid the always returning oppression of impenetrable darkness. Beth heard screams of terror echoing in her ears before becoming aware that they originated from her own throat. A roaring furnace opened immediately in front of them. The heat seemed to sear her very eyebrows as the tracks swerved away at the last minute and the flames were left behind. When they finally emerged into the blinding lights of the platform from which they had departed, she sat motionless, as if welded to the metal seats.

"Again!" Her voice emerged in a whisper from a throat parched by shrieking. "Again!"

It took both Serenity and the attendant to pull her out of the car.

"Ben was right." She grabbed Beth's hand and maneuvered her through the crowd which had just exited the Sight and Sound Cyclorama of the Red Sea Crossing. Claiming two empty seats in St. Peter's Fish Emporium, she waved a waiter over and ordered for them both. "Ben was right, and wrong. I have rewritten history. Crusaders died right along with Saracens. The Inquisition was bloody. The church would not be where it is today without its martyrs. But an amusement park needs to provide hope. You wanted to go on every ride again because you survived."

"I wanted to go on every ride again because they were thrilling."

"But if you hadn't survived? Would you have wanted to go again?"

"I guess I wouldn't have had that choice." Beth accepted the two platters of fish and chips, placed them on the small table, and paid the waiter before Serenity could object. "Would you mind telling me what all this is about? Ben was right about what? And wrong about what?"

Over their lunch Serenity shared the entire story of her visit to Leila, impromptu re-enactment of "Into the Woods" with Prince Charming, and especially the accusations he had hurled concerning her desire to rewrite history through the theme park.

"He was right about survival. But otherwise it wouldn't be amusement. Besides, remember that old gospel song we used to listen to? 'I've Read the Back of the Book and We Win.'"

"I loved that Cathedrals CD. So, Ben thinks that people should die on the theme park rides? That would be a bummer."

"Well, he never said that, although I probably accused him of such callousness. He just tried to convince me that I couldn't rewrite history. I needed to accept the past and not allow it to determine my future."

"Leave it to the two of you to discuss theme park theology. Other couples talk about Song of Solomon while you two debate the finer points of Lamentations. Maybe he wasn't talking about Spirit of the Spire at all."

"Then why did he use Descent into Hades as his prime example?"

"Has something about his past changed recently?"

Serenity tried to remember how their argument in her mother's apartment had started. She had arrived first and been looking at his resume when the nurse told her mother Prince Charming had come for a visit. The combination of staring at his smiling 8x10 glossy and the nurses' ridiculous title for a visitor had raised the anger hackles on her sensibilities as soon as he walked through the door. Prince Charming, indeed. He had never made any attempt to charm her. The ridiculous dialogue from the Sondheim musical hadn't helped. But she admitted to herself that something had been different about him. Hadn't he talked about wanting to court her, about wanting to ask since the day they first met? Wanting to ask what? There had never been any indication of interest before then. Never. Something about him had changed. Beth was right. He had been talking about rewriting his history, not hers. She owed it to herself. She owed it to him to find out what had changed.

# CHAPTER SEVENTEEN

Serenity had always loved walking into the Spire as a young girl. The shining silver exterior reminded her of a rocket ship with her father as the captain, waiting to carry them all into outer space. She would often join the tour groups led by energetic volunteers who provided visitors with their introduction to the genius behind the construction of the auditorium. She had heard the spiel so many times she could move her lips in sync with the narrators.

"The spire soars sixty-six stories above the concrete soil," the guide would announce. "One for each of the sixty-six books of the Bible. Therefore, you are now standing in Genesis. The exterior is not actually silver, Dr. Edwards doesn't take in that much money." It was a quiet joke but never failed to elicit polite laughter. "It is rather silver-tinted glass. Office space occupies the outside perimeter, necessary since the Spire employs nearly twelve hundred people. But it is the heart of the Spire where people around the world assemble to worship each week. As we step through the doors, you will recognize immediately what you have observed from afar every Sunday. It is here where the lifeblood flows."

The widened eyes, broad smiles, and involuntary gasps as the doors to the auditorium were opened never failed to fill Serenity with a sense of pride. The room revealed the prescience and innovative vision of the man she called father.

"For generations the theater has outperformed the church in lighting, costuming, designing, comfort, access, and acoustics. Nowhere has the disparity been more evident than in architecture. Theaters slant their floors so the people in the last row see something besides hairdos in disarray.

Churches leave their floors flat. Theaters focus light on the faces of the actors, while churches filter light through stained glass from behind the speaking platform so the preacher's face remains obscured. Theaters thrust their stages into the audience and circle the seating around the platform so that even those in the last seats miss no nuance of vocal or verbal expression. Churches seat people so far away that their only participation in the worship comes via loudspeakers which destroy tone quality in favor of volume. The average backseat church-goer wouldn't recognize the man he or she listened to on Sunday if they climbed into the back seat of the same taxi on Monday."

The guide would always stop as the doors opened so people could use their phones to capture a picture. Only when she had their complete attention would the lecture continue.

"With one set of visionary blueprints, however, the pendulum swung in favor of the church. The auditorium in the Silver Spire seats seventy-five thousand, and yet every seat remains within twenty feet of the platform. No audience member obscures another's view. All attention focuses on the speaker, with distractions non-existent. Circle the seats around the stage and stack them vertically so that every worshipper occupies a prime seating location. Seventeen architects refused the design until God led Dr. Edwards to one who would catch the vision. That man's reputation now ranks right along side I. M. Pei and Frank Lloyd Wright. The insurmountable problem for other designers lay in the location of the pulpit. Stacking the seats vertically increased the distance to a ground-level platform. But extending the platform vertically solved that problem. Using holographic technology, Dr. Edwards's image appears directly in front of every viewer."

The early holographic technology had long since been replaced by invisible screens mounted in front of every seat. No matter where you sat in the auditorium, you experienced a personal conversation with the speaker. In essence, the view was now the same as they received on their personal devices anywhere in the world, but people still came by the thousands to fill the Spire for Dr. Edwards's sermons and then head over to her Spirit of the Spire for the afternoon.

Today the crowd queuing up for the Silver Spire Tour appeared to be even larger than usual. The massive welcome center teemed with visitors enjoying the coffee, tea, and soft drinks provided free of charge to everyone who came into the foyer. But to Serenity, the entire sixty-six stories seemed empty. She had come almost every day after school to enjoy a cherry lemonade and then make her way up to her father's study. Her visits had been carefully blocked out on his daily calendar, a sacrosanct time, to be missed only when a schoolmate invited her to a birthday party or sleepover. Those visits now took place in a sterile hospital room rather than the comfortable environs of the library space they both so loved. He had created an alcove fitted with a small desk where she could sit and do her homework until he completed his day's work. The desk had remained even when she left for college.

The emptiness stemmed from the reality that her father would not be sitting in the familiar chair behind the desk when she arrived at his office. It had nothing to do with the fact that Ben Morris had not made an appearance in the Spire since they had left Terre Haute, she told herself. Moving quietly through the crowds in Genesis, Serenity rode up to the seventeenth floor, Esther, where a sign over the suite door read, "For such a time as this." She stopped to greet his longtime executive assistant, Verna. The buxom, grandmotherly aide rose from her desk and enveloped Serenity in a warm embrace.

"My dear. How are you holding up under this strain? Is there any improvement?"

Serenity shook her head. "I want you to know how much I appreciate your steady hand, Verna. The ministry continues to roll on like a well-oiled machine."

"And well it should. We all love your father. You tell him not to worry about a thing."

"He knows that. And so do I."

Glancing across the hall at the office usually occupied by Ben, she tried to phrase her next question casually, not admitting even to herself that there was another reason she had stopped in at the Spire. She had to know how his history had been rewritten. "Have you seen Dr. Morris this morning by any chance?"

"Not since he left for Chicago. Should I leave a message on his desk?"

"That won't be necessary. If you don't mind, I would just like to spend some time in father's study."

"You know you don't need my permission, dear. From what Attorney Wiley tells me, it will soon be yours anyway."

Serenity stopped with her hand still on the door to her father's office and turned back toward his personal assistant. The remark had sounded cynical, but she could see no evidence of negativity on Verna's face. With a quick change of plans she moved an office chair to a place in front of the desk. "I think it might be good for you to tell me exactly what Mr. Wiley has been saying."

Verna smiled. "At your service, dear. Where shall we start?"

"Wherever you deem appropriate."

"Fine. Let me begin with a question I trust you will not find impertinent. Do you plan to marry Lawrence Wiley?"

Serenity inhaled sharply and gradually expelled the air from her lungs. She might find herself engaged to Billy Wilson if he ever found time to visit her father. She speculated that perhaps Ben Morris had admitted he wanted to court her in the middle of a convoluted argument fueled by her vitriol. And now Lawrence Wiley?

"I assume you have a motive for asking that question?"

"You wanted to know what he has been saying." Verna straightened some papers on her desk, giving ample time for Serenity to respond. When nothing more was said, she proceeded with her explanation. "He's been in almost every day since the T-3 Project began. I know his name did not appear on the Project list. I prepared those dossiers myself. If you have some arrangement with him which you don't want publicized, let me know and I will cease and desist."

Serenity nodded acceptance and refusal of the offer. "Go ahead," she said.

"The day he met with you and Ben, before the trip to Afghanistan, marks the last time he has been in your father's study, in spite of the daily visits. I have kept the door to the study locked since Dr. Edwards entered the hospital. When word spread through the office complex that Daniel Ellicott and Michal DeLoran had refused consideration as possible successors to your father, Lawrence intimated to more than one of us that you had accepted a proposal from him. He never mentioned specifically that it was a proposal for marriage, but the word managed to enter into every conversation."

Serenity rested her arms on the edge of the desk, making direct eye contact with her father's most trusted employee. "Tell me this, Verna. Describe your gut reaction if Lawrence Wiley became your boss?"

Verna returned the gaze with equal intensity. "Serenity, dear. I would rather work for the Prince of Darkness himself."

"Thank you," said Serenity as she gathered up her purse. "That's all I needed to know."

## Chapter Eighteen

"Father, I need to tell you about my visit with Billy Wilson."

Sitting beside a hospital bed, talking with a man she loved, and experiencing no hope of hearing a response, qualified as the most difficult circumstance Serenity had ever faced. The inevitable comparison with her lifetime struggle to communicate with her mother only made it worse. The drip-drip of the IV, the hum of monitors, the silent entrance and exits of caregivers, and his labored breathing mirrored the visits with her mother. Since her last visit, Leila had decided to play the part of Sleeping Beauty, taking to her bed and insisting that she refused to be awakened by anything except a kiss from her prince.

"Billy may be coming to see you. That's how we left it. He fits all the qualifications. Above reproach certainly. The entire sports world thinks highly of him. He certainly seems hospitable. His chef cooks a mean sandwich. A good teacher. Gentle. None of the bravado or hutzpah you would expect from a football superstar. It's too bad St. Paul didn't say something about maturity though. I'm not sure he will ever be more than a kid at heart. Of course, there is that phrase about not being a novice, but no one would accuse him of not having experience in ministry."

Her father had always been there to listen, to advise. How could she possibly make this decision without him? She hated to observe the progress of pain, and witness the decline of vigor, but couldn't stay away. Like those interminable visits to her mother, she longed for lucidity and one more vibrant conversation. The one time his eyes had opened that morning, the words which came from a tortured throat had nothing to do with her quest or her dilemma.

"Psalm 91," he had whispered through chapped lips before closing his eyes again. Only a slight smile revealed his satisfaction as she fulfilled his request.

"He who dwells in the shelter of the Most High will rest in the shadow of the Almighty. I will say of the Lord, He is my refuge and my fortress, my God, in whom I trust."

Finishing that chapter, she had read some of her own choosing. Psalm 141, "But my eyes are fixed on you, O Sovereign Lord, in you I take refuge— do not give me over to death." Psalm 130, "Out of the depths I cry to you, O Lord. O Lord hear my voice. Let your ears be attentive to my cry for mercy." The words became her prayers and eventually her consolation. Psalm 107, "Give thanks to the Lord, for he is good; his love endures forever."

Setting her Bible aside, she reached out to take her father's hand. "Billy would do a good job, father. But so would the others. Is that what you were trying to tell me? That all of them meet Paul's qualifications just like Timothy? They all want to see others trained. Daniel needs leadership for his house churches. Michal wants to develop worship leaders. Billy calls them spiritual recruiters. And Ben?"

Had he just squeezed her hand? His breathing hadn't changed. No eye movement had occurred. But she could have sworn he added pressure to his grip.

"I haven't interviewed Ben. Not really. I suppose you want me to do that. But I know Ben. I know what he would say. He's been focused on one goal since the day we met: to continue the work you have started. I know we argue over silly things. Questions that don't really matter. Like the time he tried to convince me that if 'Fiddler on the Roof' was really Jewish, the song lyrics should have been 'Sunset, Sunrise,' since their days begin at sundown. But he's just like you, father. Absolutely convinced of the need for truth. He would help Daniel and Michal and Billy, just like you have done. The ministry would continue to be focused on communication of the truth."

She picked up her father's Bible again, this time moving from the Psalms to the Epistle to Timothy which had played such a key role in her life over the past several weeks.

Respectable.

Gentle.

Not a lover of money.

Able to teach.

Blameless.

Daniel.

Michal.

Billy.

Ben.

Paul's words fit them all. Father wouldn't have included them on the list otherwise. As she kept reading, the words of verse fourteen seemed to issue from the silent lips in the hospital bed beside her.

"You will know how people ought to conduct themselves in God's household, which is the church of the living God, the pillar and ground of the truth."

"You will know."

She could hear her father's voice as clearly as if she had been seated across from him at his desk.

"You will know."

She did know. She had always known. The pillar and ground of the truth. Truth mattered to God. Truth mattered to the church. Truth mattered to her father. Truth mattered to her. Truth would set her free.

# CHAPTER NINETEEN

"Beth, I know it's late, but I need to talk to Tony."

The Guilford's door mat read Welcome, and her best friend had always made it clear that she could visit at any time, but 11:00 p.m. still seemed to be taking undue advantage of their friendship.

"Come in, Sere. Are you all right? Has something happened to your father?"

"No. He's sedated, but still with us. Is Tony here?"

Before Beth could answer, her husband called from the living room. "Is that Serenity? Tell her to come in from the cold."

The couple had obviously been watching some late night television, ready to retire, but Tony pressed the remote button off as they entered the room.

"Something has upset you, Sere. How can I be of help?"

"I don't know. It's probably a long shot. But I need to try." As Beth resumed her place on the couch, Serenity seated herself in a nearby chair and leaned forward, intent on discovering anything Tony might know.

"I've already told Beth how Lawrence kept Ben's file from me when we first discussed the Project. He says it was a mistake, but I'm wondering if there might be something else he has kept from me. Do you, by any chance, have access to the incorporation papers for the Spire? Is that something available to you as an accountant?"

"Lawrence, huh? I think that man would withhold medicine from his own mother if he could sell it to someone else for a profit. Let's see what we can do."

Crossing the room to a small desk with a laptop, he sat down and began to open screens in quick succession.

"Your father has always prided himself on complete transparency in financial matters. Anyone, including investigative reporters, can access the monthly economic statements of the ministry. It has been his way of assuring the world of his integrity, something which has not always been true in religious history."

As Tony continued to search, Beth turned to her friend. "You've decided, haven't you. You've made your choice. Is it Ben?"

Serenity nodded. "I think I have known all along what father wanted. He would never have forced me to do something against my will, but he has done his best to arrange circumstances to make me willing."

"Hornets?" asked Beth.

"Exactly. Haven't thought about that old Thoro Harris song in years."

"One of our favorites."

She started singing, and Serenity joined in, enjoying the impromptu duet on a childhood chorus.

"The hornets persuaded them that it was best,

To go quickly and not to go slow.

God did not compel them to go 'gainst their will,

But he just made them willing to go."

"Think I've got something," Tony called when the girls were finished. "What was it that you needed to know?"

The three of them crowded around the laptop and scrolled down through the incorporation papers.

"Lawrence keeps talking about dissolution if a successor cannot be named. He told me that dissolution would grant me the control of all ministry finances, offering, of course, to continue as my personal advisor."

"Personal advisor, my foot," said Beth. "He's elevated himself to husband/manager status according to the scuttlebutt in the offices."

"I know. Verna told me. But something doesn't add up. He knows I would never consider a proposal, which, by the way, he has never offered. I'm just curious to know what the actual language of the document might have been and how that would affect the outcomes he has been describing."

Tony scrolled down the page, absorbing the legalize. "I don't see any provision for dissolution. However, there is a paragraph here concerning receivership. Apparently, your parents made arrangements for the repayment of creditors should the ministry encounter the need for debt restructuring."

"Receivership?"

"The two most common ways to deal with insolvency involve liquidation and receivership. Liquidation results in the termination of the business which could also be called dissolution. After debts are paid to creditors and shareholders, the business ceases to exist. Receivership offers a company the opportunity to recover and resume business. A court-appointed receiver restructures the business, pays off all debt, and then hands responsibility back to the directors."

Serenity leaned forward and read the final paragraphs for herself. "So, both of those options arise out of the need to pay off debts. Is the Spire in danger of insolvency, Tony?"

He laughed. "You don't even need to be an investigative reporter to answer that question. InSpire Ministries has no debt beyond upcoming weekly payrolls. Receivership and dissolution should be the last concern of any board of directors."

"Which brings us to this question," continued Serenity. "What, exactly, is Lawrence Wiley trying to do?"

"I have a wild guess," said Beth. "Does a court-appointed receiver get paid for his work in a receivership, Tony?"

"Absolutely. The receiver is paid from the assets placed in custody. In fact, the receiver's fees have priority over all other claims."

"Thought so," said Beth. "Isn't there some phrase in Timothy Three about not being a lover of money? Guess you can remove wily Wiley from the list he was never on in the first place."

"There's something else interesting about his document," added Tony. "You said that Lawrence initially kept back information concerning the inclusion of Ben Morris on your father's Project list?"

"He claims it was just an oversight, but yes, Ben's dossier wasn't included in the first files he gave me."

"Did he ever give you a complete copy of the T-3 Plan itself?"

"Not that I remember."

"I think you probably need to read the entire document. It could be a game changer."

As Serenity took a seat in front of the computer and began to read, the first word that captured her attention was 'Addendum.' The more she read, the more she realized how prophetic Tony's prediction might prove. Lawrence had kept back more than Ben's file. Recalling Billy's message about confidence and a change in momentum in sports contests urged her into action. This was a game changer indeed.

# CHAPTER TWENTY

Serenity's fifth grade teacher had once written a very honest evaluation on her report card, according to her father.

"Your daughter gets in trouble because she can't wait for the rest of the class to understand what she has already grasped," had been the teacher's analysis.

Her father had laughed when he read it and joked that he probably needed to change her name to Tornado. He still insisted on calling the wildest ride in the Spirit of the Spire "Serenity's Tornado." Now that she knew her own mind, she couldn't wait to bring everyone else up to speed. Phil needed to rearrange Billy's schedule and get him back to Kansas City on the double. A phone call set that plan into motion. There wasn't time for another trip to Kandahar, so a video-call would have to suffice. Verna made those arrangements. Michal had already contacted her about coming to see her father in the hospital, making his arrival imminent. That just left Ben.

He wasn't in his office. According to Verna he hadn't been seen in the Spire since the trip to Chicago. Melvin and Ashley hadn't flown him anywhere; in fact, they were grounded because Ashley had gone into labor. Her husband Jerome had taken her into the hospital, and Uncle Mel gleefully shared the news that his nephew was the one the doctors were threatening to sedate.

Ben seemed to have disappeared like the hologram of the Fallen Angels in Descent into Hades. Finally, she called his mother and heard those words no one ever wants to hear when they are looking for someone who is missing.

"I think we had better talk in person," said Ricci.

To Serenity's great surprise, when she arrived at the Alameda Towers, Ricci had company. Tyler Ravenel greeted her at the door with a warm handshake before Ben's mother enveloped her in a comforting hug.

"I didn't know you were in town, Tyler. Have you come to see father?"

"We have been at the hospital, Serenity. I know how hard it must be for you to see him in that condition. I sense that his mind still ponders the mysteries of eternity while at the same time his body clings but faintly to time. If John the Revelator hadn't forbidden any addition to the inspired scriptures, your father would be my first candidate for inclusion in the faith chapter of the epistle to the Hebrews. We both love him dearly."

The second use of the word 'we' alerted her to the realization that Tyler Ravenel, whom she had known since childhood, and Ricci Morris were....

"A couple? The two of you?"

Ricci smiled. "I know. I can't get used to the idea myself. I keep telling Ty that people will talk if we announce the engagement too soon. It seems so sudden. They won't understand that we have known each other for many years. You want to know what has happened to Ben. But before I tell you, there's something else you need to understand. Please, come and sit down."

The formal living room in the condominium looked like a display set from Chip and Joanna Gaines's *Magnolia Journal*. Double French doors beyond revealed a cluttered study area far more fitting to Serenity's concept of how a writer's workshop might appear. Her admiration for Ben's mother increased when Ricci noticed her gaze going toward the study and didn't get up to shut the doors. Ben had never been one to hide his jumbled thought process behind a formal ministerial façade either. He had once told her that the Apostle John had been described as both a burning and a shining light. You can't burn without some messy residue, had been his conclusion.

Tyler's first words made it sound like he had been reading her mind.

"I guess you could say that our first meeting was pretty messy. As a grad assistant I should have known better. She wasn't in any of my classes, so it didn't rise to the level of abuse of power. But she was still an undergraduate, so it was definitely my fault."

Ricci took his hand in her own and shook her head slightly. "We've had this discussion before, Serenity. People like to play the blame game or claim that the fault was in the stars, but we were both wrong. It shouldn't have happened, but it did."

"Then she just disappeared. I knew it hadn't been a dream, but I didn't even know her last name. I had no way to find her."

"My roommate had been sworn to secrecy and actually kept her promise. Probably the first time she ever managed to do so."

Serenity tried to wrap her mind around what they were telling her in this strange story. Grad assistant? Undergraduate? Roommate? How long ago had all this happened? This was Ben's mother. Did she have another child before Ben? What did all of this have to do with Ben disappearing?

"When your father offered to introduce me to the author of the Ric Morris novels, I was thrilled. But imagine my reaction when Ric turned out to be Ricci and I looked into the eyes of the woman I had been seeking for thirty years."

"I couldn't have written a better happy-ever-after ending myself," said Ricci. "In fact, it proved the old adage about truth being stranger than fiction. If I did write such an ending, no one would ever believe it."

Something finally clicked in Serenity's mind as all the facts she had been absorbing merged into one. They were talking about Ben. Their story concerned him and not just the two of them.

"You're Ben's father? Tyler?"

"That's what we've been trying to tell you," said Ricci. "For two fairly intelligent people, I guess we didn't provide a very coherent explanation. Both of our minds have been somewhat preoccupied for the last couple weeks."

"You mean you just found out?"

Ricci nodded. "The day before your father went into the hospital. Introducing us may have been one of the last things he ever did."

"And one of the best."

Serenity watched as Tyler wrapped his arm around Ben's mother. Ben's mother. Ben's father. Tyler Ravenel was Ben's father. What a shock that must have been for Ben.

"What can I say? Congratulations seems trite. Awesome, perhaps? Incredible? Overwhelming? Mind-blowing?"

"We've settled on overwhelming for the time being," grinned Tyler. "Awesome will happen when I finally see her coming down the aisle like a bride adorned for her husband. We wanted your father to officiate, but we realize that won't happen. So, we asked Ben to do the honors instead."

Ben! Re-writing history. What could be a greater manuscript revision than to discover your father at thirty years of age. He had told her that history could be rewritten if past history facts proved to be false.

"When did you tell him?" She knew she sounded rude, like she was making a demand instead of asking a question. But she had to know. "When did you tell Ben?"

"The same day you flew back from Denver. Why? What's the matter, Serenity?"

The day of their "Into the Woods" confrontation. He had been trying to tell her, and she wouldn't listen. His entire life story had changed. History had been rewritten, and she wouldn't listen. It was all her fault.

"Where is he, Mrs. Morris? Please. I have to see him."

"I think we can manage that. Tyler, would you switch on the television. The service should be just about to start."

As the large screen TV brightened, Serenity expected to see the familiar opening sequence for the InSpire service. Ben often spoke in her father's place, and with Dr. Edwards in the hospital that would not be unusual. Instead the words "livestream" appeared. She saw an unfamiliar platform, empty except for a lighted announcement screen welcoming those in the auditorium to Clear Creek Church. The empty stage soon filled with a group of young people who moved quietly into place facing the audience. First in unison, and then by means of solo and ensemble voices, they shared words from Psalm 145.

"I will extol thee, my God, O king; and I will bless thy name forever and ever."

As they spoke, understanding of the scripture became clear in the minds of listeners. Sitting there in the Morris living room, Serenity grasped the intent of the psalmist who had been inspired to write, "My mouth will speak in praise of the Lord."

Blended worship, ancient hymn tunes with contemporary flavor, followed seamlessly. Having attended the Spire all her life where worship music had been avoided, she found herself drawn into praise and exaltation in a way she had seldom experienced. Not until a man stood up to introduce Ben as the speaker for the day did she realize what they were watching

"He's candidating," she said, more to herself than to Ricci and Tyler.

Appearing completely at ease in what had to be a nerve-wracking situation, in front of an unfamiliar crowd intent not just on hearing him preach but on evaluating his content, style and delivery, Ben spoke clearly and confidently. Although he stood behind a pulpit, the conversational tone soon convinced all those in attendance of his desire to share a story with them, one-on-one.

"Mary grew more excited that day the closer she and Joseph approached to the temple. Forty days had passed since her son had been born. The time had come for her purification according to the law of Moses, as well as the presentation of her child to God. Surely this would be the day when the priests in the temple recognized his importance. This would be the day when holy men would come to understand what she had been pondering in her heart since the visit of the shepherds and their report of the angelic announcement. Certainly, if anyone would recognize a child sent from God, it would be the priests."

Unable to stay confined behind the pulpit, Ben walked down off the platform and approached those in the front pews.

"Mary and Joseph walked through the busy streets of Jerusalem unnoticed. Arrogant Roman soldiers on horses pushed them aside. Pharisees and Levites hurried past without even a sideways glance. At the large open Court of the Women, they experienced their first close-up view of the holy temple itself. The golden edifice, crowned with spikes which caught the glint of the sun, seemed to burn like living flames of fire. A pillar of smoke ascended into the clear blue sky from an altar in front of the Holy Place. The time of the morning sacrifice. At the edge of the Court of the Women a white-robed line of priests accepted the sacrifices of purification. Mary and Joseph joined the worshippers in awe, waiting for their turn to dedicate two small pigeons as an offering of praise to Jehovah.

"Surely now they will see the child," she thought. "They will know the truth about my babe."

As if recreating the scene for those in the auditorium, Ben walked through the aisles, speaking personally to individuals as he moved.

"Instead, the priests ignored them, looked right past them, and eagerly accepted the gifts of those bringing lambs. Only poor people brought turtledoves or pigeons. Disheartened, Joseph pulled her close to his side as they joined others also being forced aside to wait. Finally, when there were no more lambs, the priests quickly gathered all the birds and carried them toward the altar. Joseph gently took the child from Mary's arms and followed them, leaving her behind in the court, the only location in the temple accessible to women. What had begun as a day of rejoicing had degenerated into a morass of despondency. Not a single priest or Levite in all the temple had recognized her child, her son sent from God."

Back on the platform, he reached out his arms to receive the infant as if he were Simeon.

"The sacrifice complete, Joseph rejoined her, handing her their precious bundle, and turning to go. But an old man blocked their way. Plucking the child from the arms of his mother, he began to pray."

"'Sovereign Lord, as you have promised, now dismiss your servant in peace. For my eyes have seen your salvation which you have prepared in the sight of all people, a light for revelation to the Gentiles and for glory to your people Israel.'"

"Before the old man had finished his prayer, a woman over eighty years of age joined in, calling out to all who would listen her words of praise to God for this one who had come to redeem his people."

As Ben shared the story of Simeon and Anna from the gospel of Luke, Serenity watched the rapt faces of those who sat in the chairs at Clear Creek Church. Under no possible conditions would they refuse to accept such a man as their pastor. She had waited too long to make up her mind.

# CHAPTER TWENTY-ONE

Early the next morning, after a sleepless night, Serenity sought solace in one of her favorite venues in the theme park, the Hall of History: Voices from the Past.

Normally the small auditorium overflowed with parents seeking relief from the high-octane rides so loved by their children. Most of them would return later with their families in tow, thrilled by the voices they had heard and anxious to introduce their heirs to religious history.

Today she sat alone in the semidarkness, having instructed the attendant to post a "Temporarily Closed" sign on the entrance.

Voices from the Past had proved even riskier than most of the attractions her fertile mind conceived for the Spirit of the Spire. Also, one of the most expensive. Recreating historical sermons involved hiring actors, but also costumers, make-up artists, speech coaches, lighting designers, and scene painters. In order to create historically accurate scenarios, the filming included extras, sometimes numbering into the hundreds, all in authentic period dress. The forty-eight-minute presentation on the big screen included twenty-four two-minute excerpts from famous sermons, each one captured from a viewpoint which included the audience in the theater as part of the crowd originally listening to the preacher.

Peter on the day of Pentecost. You experienced the thrill of witnessing words which compelled over three thousand people to repent and turn to God.

Paul on Mars Hill. As one of the skeptic Athenians, you heard his proclamation of the unknown God.

Polycarp, who facing condemnation to burning at the stake, declared "Eighty-six years have I served him, and he has done me no wrong How can I blaspheme my King and my Savior?"

Chrysostom, the Golden-mouthed orator of Antioch.

Martin Luther's speech at the Imperial Diet in Worms, 1521.

All appeared in person, speaking their own words, immersed in the culture, surroundings, and physical trappings of the time period in which they lived. Living history.

Martyrs, Savonarola and Wycliff.

Theologians, Augustine and Calvin.

Missionaries, John Wesley and David Brainerd.

Pulpiteers, Jonathan Edwards and Charles Spurgeon.

Evangelists, D. L. Moody, Billy Sunday, and Billy Graham.

The risk had paid off with Voices from the Past quickly becoming one of the theme park venues requiring advance reservations for admittance. The final two minutes carried the audience into the familiar environs of the Spire as they listened to Dr. Ernst Edwards expound on the challenge of the Lord to Moses at the burning bush. "What is that in thy hand?" It was the sermon that inspired many of the Freedom Projects, including her own vision for the Spirit of the Spire.

She knew exactly when he entered and sat down in the row behind her. She would have known even without the slight squeak of the door hinges, the temporary flash of light from the foyer, and the swish of shoes on the floor. How often had she sensed his presence in the past, even when he blended into the background trying to appear inconspicuous?

The fact that he wanted her to know he was there became obvious when his familiar baritone blended with the onscreen pronouncement of Augustine, "You have made us for yourself, O Lord, and our hearts are restless until they rest in you."

It was a game they had played during the writing of the script for Voices. Asking for his advice had escalated into competition, trying to recall which historical quotes might be the most memorable, which words people would leave the theater repeating in their minds. Attempting to capture the essence of twenty-four preachers in the space of two-minute excerpts provided ample fuel for their amiable and sometimes contrary discussions. Somehow, sitting in the dark, the words he chose to repeat assumed even greater significance.

Savonarola, opposing the tyranny and corruption of the Medici in Florence, spoke passionately from the pulpit of the Convent of San Marco, surrounded by his supporters from the city. On the edges of the crowd stood the scowling Arrabbiati who would soon persuade the Duke of Milan and Pope Alexander to hang him and burn his body. The passionate words from behind her joined the martyr's voice at the very end of the clip. "Do you want to be free? Then above all things, love God, love your neighbor, love one another; then you will have true liberty."

Love one another? Could that be his message to her? Or was he simply reminding her of their earlier sparring over the choice of famous quotes?

His synchronous citation with John Wesley, preaching to coal miners in the open fields near Bristol, England, after being banned from London pulpits, seemed more retrospective. "Beware you be not swallowed up in books! An ounce of love is worth a pound of knowledge."

Wesley criticized the religious leaders of his day who focused on scholarship and ignored the needs of the common people like coal miners. Was Ben admitting a shortcoming of his own? Focusing on his knowledge and ignoring love?

"I have a secret thought from some things I have observed, that God may perhaps design you for some singular service in the world." Missionary David Brainerd's address to the Delaware Indians of New Jersey took on new meaning when uttered with baritone delivery in a darkened theater. But was he talking about her service, or his? Was this an attempt to explain the candidacy at Clear Creek?

The rapid progress of the Voices presentation would have prevented extensive conversation even if she had been inclined to turn around and confront him. His voice blended with that of David Livingstone in the jungles along the Zambezi River of Central Africa. "I am prepared to go anywhere, provided it be forward."

Evangelist D. L. Moody, preaching to 30,000 at the Botanic Gardens Palace in Glasgow, Scotland, said, "Faith makes all things possible. Love makes all things easy." Serenity heard the same words in an entirely different context, a darkened room with only two occupants.

Pulpiteer Charles Haddon Spurgeon electrified the overflow crowd at the Metropolitan Tabernacle in London as he thundered out a warning. "Beware of no man more than of yourself; we carry our worst enemies within us." The same words, spoken concurrently in quiet, conversational tones, struck her as more apology than warning.

The sequence of Jim Elliot, still a student at Wheaton College, speaking to a small group of his fellow wrestlers far in advance of his death on the banks of the Curaray River in Ecuador, 1956, never failed to stir her emotions. Hearing the familiar words quoted by Ben along with Elliot increased the intensity of her reaction beyond her ability to maintain control. "God always gives his best to those who leave the choice with him."

The tears began to flow. As her father's familiar face filled the screen, she felt his arms surround her. Not her father's arms, but Ben's. The man she had refused to admit she loved even more than she loved her father.

The lights brightened. A pre-recorded voice reminded viewers to check around their seats for personal items which might be left behind. They were asked to exit toward the front of the room so that others could enter from the back. Serenity and Ben obeyed as the attendant removed the "temporarily closed" sign and eager park goers rushed into the space which had for a short time been their own private retreat.

A bench along the boulevard across from the Whirlwind of Elijah's Chariot provided no respite from the throngs of park visitors streaming by. But to them it might as well have been Simeon Stylite's platform on top of a pillar in the desert near Aleppo, Syria. For several minutes they sat silently, holding hands but unsure where to begin.

"I heard your sermon at Clear Creek," Serenity broke the ice.

"Mother told me you were at the house. I wanted to tell you before I went."

"It's a great opportunity for you. I know you will do well."

"Would you believe me if I told you I did it for both of us?"

She shrugged slightly. "You've never lied to me before. But I don't think I understand."

"The words in the theater. I meant them all, Sere. I guess I've been like Christian in Cyrano de Bergerac. Looking for someone else to write what I should have been saying all along."

"Speak for yourself, sir," Serenity whispered, remembering the words of Roxanne.

"I have always loved you. The day of my interview, when your father so graciously invited me into his study, and you reluctantly left your books behind so we could be alone. I had no idea you came there every night after school rather than returning to an empty house. I just knew that you had a beautiful countenance and a quick wit."

"Don't forget the sharp tongue. That was the night father introduced you as the young man who read from the original Greek and Hebrew during devotions, and I said…"

"Does he sing in Illyrian and text in Etruscan?"

"You remember."

"I've never forgotten. Amazement at your awareness of Indo-European languages was exceeded only by the memory of eyes that sparkled with their own private whimsy, a vibrant personality too substantial to be confined to such a delicate frame, and…"

"A smart lip that disfigured an otherwise charming visage?"

"You're putting words in my mouth."

"Apparently I should have been shoving them between your teeth years ago. You've never said anything in all these years to suggest an interest. You wouldn't even admit you were part of the T-3 Project."

"I have to admit that I was thankful when I first learned that the lawyer had failed to give you my file. I thought that perhaps the trip to Afghanistan would provide some time to talk without the specter of the succession interfering. From the day your father first proposed the Project, I knew it would create tension for the two of us. If you felt in any way coerced to marry me for the sake of the ministry, you would always wonder if you had made the right choice. If I asked you to marry me at any time during the process, you would wonder whether I loved the Spire more than you."

"And if I awarded the prize of succession to the man I loved, he would never know if my decision came from loyalty to father or what Savonarola called 'true liberty.' We know each other too well."

"Which led me to my decision concerning Clear Creek. I have no intention of going there alone. I want you with me, as my wife. I want you to know that my love for you in no way depends upon anything connected to your father's ministry. As much as I admire what he has done and long for it to endure and prosper, my love for you exceeds that longing as the mighty Pacific exceeds the little Galilee Pond you installed here at the park, and keep stocked with guppies so children can pretend to be Peter, James, and John in a sailboat."

"You never did like that pond." Serenity gazed at the crowds passing by without really seeing any of them. The temptation to leave it all behind, to walk into an unseen future alongside this man who loved her more than fame and fortune, to believe that God always gives his best to those who leave the choice with him, grew strong. One great question remained.

"Why now?" she said, turning away from her dream land to face him directly. "There were years before the T-3 Project when you could have approached me without the specter of succession looming. Why was it necessary to play Lancelot and 'love me once in silence?' It wasn't as if I was married to King Arthur. You've known every fellow I ever dated. I would have listened. Regardless of my sharp tongue and smart lip, I have wanted to do more than spar mentally with you. Why did you wait?"

"'We carry our worst enemies within us.' Spurgeon knew exactly what he was talking about. You'll never know how much I longed to court you, to break the silence. But there was a reason. Can we walk?" Offering his hand, he pulled her to her feet and then looped his arm through hers as they strolled slowly along with the crowd.

"Your father?" She said after another long silence.

"You knew?"

"Not till yesterday. Tyler Ravenel. You must be very pleased."

"Beyond delighted, verging on over the moon. I haven't known much longer than that myself."

"They told me. You found out the day we went 'Into the Woods.'"

Ben stopped walking. A thoughtful smile revealed his pleasure at her apt description of their argument. "I wanted you to be the first to know."

"That history had been rewritten."

"Exactly. Did they tell you what he said? 'At the risk of sounding like a puny imitation of Darth Vader, I must tell you, Ben. I am your father.' Luke Skywalker couldn't have been more shocked than I was. Until then, I had no idea of my past. Oh, I knew my mother and loved her. I kept telling myself her love should have been enough. But it wasn't. You can laugh if you want, but I spent over a year translating the four books of the Kings from the Hebrew, trying to find some pattern in the word choice of the author. A wicked king would sometimes sire a good son, but far more often those who turned away from God spawned offspring even more evil than themselves."

"You know it wouldn't have mattered. Every son of every king made a personal choice. I never harbored any doubt that you had made yours."

"I tried to convince myself of that intellectual reality many times. But mother wouldn't talk about it except to say that my father didn't know. From that I assumed that he didn't care. When Tyler shared their story, I felt like Bunyan's Pilgrim losing his heavy burden as it rolled off his back and into the mouth of the sepulchre. I was free."

"And I wouldn't listen."

"It wasn't your fault. Let's stay out of those woods. My pride still would not allow me to make the most horrible confession of all. Because I didn't know my father, my imagination had sometimes run wild. I still hesitate to tell you this, but I am learning that only the truth can set us free." Ben paused in the middle of the busy piazza and embraced her warmly before continuing.

"How long have your folks been married, Sere?"

"You know that. We just celebrated their thirtieth anniversary."

"Right. And I'm thirty-one. Please forgive me, but my greatest fear has been the baseless worry that the reason mother wouldn't reveal my father's name had something to do with Dr. Edwards. He's never given me any reason to think poorly of him in all the years I have known him. The entire idea proved abhorrent to me, and yet it lingered, vexed, chafed my conscience, and erected a great wall I found impossible to scale every time I thought about declaring my love. I possessed no evidence aside from the fact that my birth occurred before your parents got married. The thought, once conceived, took root, grew faster than a field of sunflowers, and refused to be uprooted. All of that changed the day I learned the name of my father."

Right in the middle of the path, Serenity pulled his face down to hers and initiated a loving kiss. It lasted so long that people began to stop and stare, some even taking pictures on their cell phones. Finally, she stepped away and grabbed his hand, forcing him to race beside her like the White Rabbit and Alice toward the closest exit.

"I think it's time we paid another visit to my mother, Prince Charming."

# CHAPTER TWENTY-TWO

As soon as they exited the elevator on her mother's floor, Serenity sensed something wrong. The Disney soundtrack which always greeted Leila's visitors with cheery, fairy tale tunes had gone silent. Rushing past the nurse in the outer hospital room, she sank to her knees beside the colorful quilt replete with images of Snow White, Cinderella, Sleeping Beauty, and Ariel.

"Mother. Sleeping Beauty. I've brought him. Prince Charming is here. It's time to wake up, mother. Everyone in the castle has come back to life. There's going to be a wedding. Please, mother. Please wake up."

She felt her mother's wrist and then laid a hand on her temple, brushing back the strands of hair that drifted over the side of her face. Leaning over, she placed a cheek against her lips, anxiously trying to sense evidence of the breath of life and finding none.

"Camilla," the urgency in Serenity's voice brought Leila's nurse on the run. "She's not breathing. We must do something. She can't be gone. She can't."

The nurse tried. A doctor joined the endeavor. But to no avail. With a smile on her face, Leila had concluded her life story awaiting the kiss of her prince.

Ben stayed close as the doctor gently led Serenity through the process of providing the information for the death certificate. Age, race, sex, date of birth, birthplace, time of death—cold facts that didn't even begin to reveal the essence of the person whose life had ceased to exist. Questions about funeral parlors and burial sites. Who would be alerted to collect the body? Cause of death? Information requested by the government or by faceless researchers planning or funding programs designed to analyze, reduce, or prevent mortality.

They had completed less then half the pages of questions when Serenity abruptly pushed back her chair and looked around for her purse.

"Father. We're going to have to finish this later. I need to tell my father."

The trip to the hospital seemed to require a new description for the concept of molasses in January, perhaps stagnant in the dog days of summer. Every stoplight glowed red. Every driver traveled in a torpid daydream, refusing to accelerate even to the lowest level of the speed limit. Ben honked and swerved, hoping for one of those fictional rescues where an indulgent policeman takes pity and leads people through traffic with a screaming siren. Instead, the sixteen-minute journey took nearly half an hour. Dropping Serenity off at the door, he threw his keys toward a valet and raced after her toward the now familiar intensive treatment ward.

Two doctors and multiple nurses crowded around the bed. As they pushed on the door, one of the nurses tried to prevent it from opening before recognizing Serenity. The doctors stood near the window in consultation as nurses efficiently performed the necessary procedures to detach the sensors, IVs, monitors, and medical paraphernalia which had been providing the tenacious lifelines binding Dr. Edwards to continued vitality.

For the second time that morning, Serenity bore the burden of providing cold facts concerning a precious life. When the doctor recorded the time of death, she turned to Ben, and the tears began to flow. Somehow Leila had known. The bonds of love had become the bonds of death. The time of death on both certificates read 11:04.

# CHAPTER TWENTY-THREE

T he summons from Burnley, Wiley, and Associates arrived via
special messenger, a functionary of the law firm who had tracked
Serenity down as she shared the news of her father's death with his
administrative assistant, Verna.

"Grass doesn't grow under the feet of Old Scratch," observed Verna
when the messenger had closed the door behind him.

"You've been invited to a meeting in the office of Dr. Ernst Edwards
at 9:00 a.m. tomorrow morning concerning the resolution of the Timothy
Three Project," read Serenity. "We need to give him the benefit of the doubt,
Verna. He's just trying to do his job."

"Well, his job will never be my job. He doesn't even have the decency
to wait until after the funerals. Do you want me to lock the door to the
study so he has to request the key?"

"That won't be necessary. Just arrange five chairs in a semicircle away
from the desk, and make certain the Zoom contact is functioning for our
special guest from Kandahar."

"At least grant me permission to remove your father's chair from behind the desk. Asmodeus doesn't deserve to occupy that position."

Serenity smiled. "That you may have my permission to do. Just be sure
to address him as Lawrence tomorrow, and not Lucifer."

"I'll try, Serenity. I will certainly try."

When Lawrence Wiley entered the office suite of Dr. Edwards at 8:45
the next morning, the door to the study stood open. Failing to find the pad-
ded swivel desk chair which normally sat behind the large oak workstation,
he pulled one of the smaller chairs into that position, re-situating the others

so they faced the desk. If he became aware of the icy glare from the other room, he chose to ignore it.

"Good morning, sir," Verna greeted him. "May I bring you a cup of coffee."

"Won't be necessary. This shouldn't take long. May I ask why five chairs at a meeting to which only Miss Edwards has been invited?"

"You may," said Verna, returning to her desk without elaborating further.

Billy Wilson arrived next, accompanied by his linemen. Deke and Phil tossed a football back and forth, while at the same time exploring the hundreds of books lining the walls. Billy leaned over the desk to offer a handshake to the lawyer.

"Mr. Wiley, I presume? Names Billy Wilson. Thanks for that letter you sent about the T-3 Project. Sure had a great visit with Ms. Edwards, didn't we, boys? She conducts a mean interview."

Lawrence stood, ignoring the handshake, and tried to step out from behind the desk only to find his way blocked by two linebackers, each outweighing him by a hundred pounds. They were casually tossing the football back and forth over his head, dropping it lower on each pass until he finally resumed his seat. "Mr. Wilson. I would be glad to arrange a meeting with you later this morning. But this happens to be a private conference, so please take your football buddies and excuse yourself."

"Concerning the T-3 Project, right? Well, I happen to be part of that project according to the letter I received from your firm."

Before Wiley could manage a reply, Michal DeLoran made his entrance. At the same time, Verna pressed the remote and the image of Daniel Ellicott appeared on the screen. "Looks like we're all here except Serenity and Ben," said Michal. "Good to see you again, Billy. Toss it over here and go out for a pass, Deke."

As the football flew from Deke to Michal and back to Deke again, Lawrence began to sputter. "What is going on here? You're not the Prophet."

Michal caught the football handily, and this time he launched it in the direction of Phil. "Absolutely right, Mr. Wiley. Not the Prophet. But I am Michal DeLoran. Thanks for your letter."

"My thanks as well," said the voice of Daniel Ellicott via Zoom. "Greetings to all of you. I assume Ben and Serenity have been detained?"

Verna stood in the doorway, beaming over the controlled chaos in the study, and especially the look of utter frustration on the face of the lawyer.

"Ben's secretary called him to the phone for an urgent message. They are right across the hall in his office. Should be here momentarily. Go right ahead with your ball game, fellows."

"Catch, Daniel," yelled Phil, throwing the football directly at the screen only to have Billy intercept it as Ben and Serenity came into the room.

"Deke? Phil? I don't think Mr. Wiley provided enough seating for the two of you. Perhaps it would be best if you took your game into Verna's office," said Serenity.

"Would someone tell me what is going on here?" Lawrence's voice trembled as he watched the two linebackers exit along with Dr. Edwards's administrative assistant, who deliberately left the door between the two offices ajar.

"It's your meeting, Mr. Wiley. I guess you'll have to be the one to answer that," replied Serenity.

"A private meeting, if you recall. My invitation was issued only to you."

"I do recall. The summons specifically mentioned the resolution of the T-3 Project. Providentially, all those men involved in the plan happened to be in town, and Daniel has been able to join us remotely due to the marvels of the technological age in which we live. Greetings, Daniel. It is so good to see you again."

"Thank you, Serenity. Let me share my condolences on the death of your parents. My heart grieves with you, knowing what a burden it must be to deal with legal matters concurrently with preparations for their funerals. Wouldn't you agree, Mr. Wiley?"

"Of course," coughed Lawrence. "Miss Edwards has my condolences as well. But it is because of the untimely death of her parents that the law firm of Burnley, Wiley, and Associates finds it necessary to proceed in this manner. It is of the utmost importance that we resolve this matter promptly."

"And what matter might that be?" asked Serenity.

"Very well." Lawrence retrieved a document from his breast pocket and unfolded it on the desk. "I am under obligation to inform you that the Honorable Judge Mateo Diego of the United States District Court for the District of Kansas has appointed a receiver for the oversight of Receivership for the totality of InSpire Ministries. His assigned task includes restructuring the business, paying off all debt, and then handing responsibility back to the directors. Since by virtue of the death of Dr. and Mrs. Edwards you are the only remaining director, the adjudication of this consideration pertains only to you."

"I see." Serenity looked around at the others in the room, as well as Daniel on the big screen, a miniscule smile flirting with one end of her mouth. "A couple of questions if I may."

"Certainly."

"I assume the judge has been apprised of the financial situation of the ministry, since his edict makes reference to the payment of debt?"

"It will be the sole responsibility of the Receiver to determine the extent of indebtedness incurred by the corporation."

"In other words, the judge was not apprised of any specific financial considerations?"

"He concluded that the reduction of the board of governors to a single individual warranted an investigation regardless of prior financial reportage."

"I see. So, this is not really a financial matter. It relates instead to the arrangements for succession in the original incorporation papers. And am I to assume that someone from your law firm will be serving as Receiver?"

"Burnley, Wiley, and Associates concluded that because of our prior association and the previous discussions we have conducted concerning the dissolution of the ministry assets, it would be best for all concerned if I assumed that legal responsibility. Your father has trusted Burnley and Associates since the earliest days of the ministry. It will be our deliberative objective to bring about restructuring and restoration as expeditiously as is legally possible in order not to impede your vision for the future of your father's ministry."

Serenity slid the judicial orders off the desk, read them carefully, and then handed them to Ben, who glanced over them and passed them on to Michal and Billy. The sports evangelist held them up to the camera on the computer screen so Daniel could see them as well.

Rather than resuming her seat, Serenity began to pace the room, as if she were questioning a witness in front of a jury of his peers. "Since this entire matter concerns succession and not financial matters, which according to our accountant could not be better, perhaps your firm should return to Judge Diego and inform him that receivership will not be necessary. Succession has already been determined."

Lawrence placed a hand to his forehead and sighed. "Serenity, don't make this harder on yourself. I know you are distraught over your father's death. I know your desire above all is to please him. But don't be foolish. Legal oversight in the form of receivership will provide you the wise counsel, as well as sufficient time, to avoid any spur-of-the-moment decision you may one day come to regret. I know all about the proposal of Billy Wilson, but his five minute homilies will never satisfy the millions of listeners who have come to depend on your father for their spiritual nourishment."

Billy's grin could have lit up an entire stadium without artificial lighting. "So, you heard about that did you? Deke and Phil will be proud of the rumors they planted. Nothing would please me more than actual engagement to Serenity Edwards, but all of us knew from the beginning that Dr. Edwards's goals for the T-3 Plan never involved proposals of marriage. He would never have placed his daughter in such a predicament. If you want to know the truth about succession, you will have to look to someone else besides me."

Serenity placed the judge's order back on the desk. Slipping her arm around Ben's waist, she pulled him next to her side and whispered something in his ear.

Ben kissed her on the cheek and then turned to face the row of chairs and the screen, their backs to the lawyer.

"Dr. Benjamin Morris would like to take this opportunity to announce his engagement to Miss Serenity Edwards, daughter of the late Dr. and Mrs. Ernst Edwards."

Daniel began to applaud on screen. Michal and Billy alternated back-slapping and handshakes for Ben with enthusiastic hugs for Serenity. Deke, Phil, and Verna joined them as Lawrence sat like a granite bust behind the desk. Gradually his visage morphed into a sinister sneer.

"Well played, Miss Edwards. However, I must remind you that the incorporation papers require a unanimous decision by a three-person board for any major decision. Unless you and Morris already have a bun in the oven…"

Before he could finish the sentence, Billy leap-frogged the desk and slammed him up against the wall. Deke and Phil barreled across the room to join the attack, intent on adding another quarterback sack to their resumes. Lawrence curled up like an armadillo, or as Deke later described him, a dung beetle, but Serenity came to the rescue before they could do any real damage.

"Leave him be fellows. He's not worth the effort. The ministry no longer has any need for his services."

"You can't fire me," Lawrence blustered as the three football giants released him and he sunk back down into the chair."

"She doesn't have to," said Daniel. "I'll do it."

"And so will I," added Michal.

"It would be my pleasure," agreed Ben.

"As well as mine," said Billy. "You would think that a lawyer adept at writing the small print would also read it. But then again, perhaps you did read it and chose to obfuscate, the way you have done with the rest of the T-3 Project. Not only did you fail to inform Serenity of Ben's participation in the Project. Not only did you give us the false impression that succession to the ministry required matrimony on her part. You also neglected to mention in any of your letters that all those who, in her estimation, fit the biblical qualifications listed by the Apostle Paul would automatically become permanent members of the official administrative board of InSpire."

"None of this changes the order from Judge Diego in any way. I have been entrusted with authority which takes precedence over any administrative entities. You can make any claim you wish, but this document stands as self-evident truth."

Lawrence had regained some of his bluster, but shriveled physically when Deke took a short step in his direction. This time Daniel took control of the floor.

"Strange that you should use that word, Mr. Wiley. I have been reading an account of a class in mental philosophy taught by President Harrison Webster of Union College. He asked a student to define self-evident, something the student proved incapable of doing. So he proceeded to illustrate in the following fashion. 'Speaking about mythology,' said President Webster, 'suppose I should ask you if there ever was such a person as a fool killer? What would be your reply?' Would you care to respond to that question, Mr. Wiley?"

"How ridiculous. Of course, there's no such person. It's mythology. I've never met one."

"Exactly." Daniel leaned closer to the camera so his face completely filled the screen. "That is self-evident."

"The duly appointed board of InSpire Ministries will present a response to Judge Diego yet this afternoon, along with a certified audit from our accountant, Tony Guilford, proving that the financial status of the ministry involves no indebtedness and is therefore exempt from any need for foreclosure, bankruptcy, or receivership." Serenity walked behind the desk as she spoke, gesturing for Lawrence to vacate her father's chair, something he agreed to only when once again approached by Deke and Phil. "We will also remind him that court-appointed receivers must be independent parties with no prior business relationship to either a borrower or a lender. I am certain he will quickly withdraw his illegal order when faced with the facts you have obviously withheld from him when asking for this ruling. Deke? Phil? Would you be so kind as to escort Mr. Wiley from the building since his services are no longer required by this ministry?"

Lawrence reached for the court document only to discover that it had disappeared from the top of the desk and rested firmly in the hands of Benjamin Morris.

"Come along, Larry," said Phil. "Can I call you Larry? I feel as if we have become so well acquainted in the past few minutes."

"Would you like to go out for a pass?" suggested Deke. "It would give us a reason to tackle you."

"No tackling," laughed Serenity. "Just get him out of the building safely."

As they passed through the outer office, it was Verna who got in the last word. "Goodbye Luc...Um. Goodbye, Lawrence."

The atmosphere within the study of Dr. Ernst Edwards transformed almost immediately from gloom to glee. Once Deke and Phil had escorted Wiley from the building, the business of the board moved forward rapidly. Billy and Michal volunteered to deliver the decision concerning receivership to His Honor the Judge. Daniel nominated Ben as the successor to Dr. Edwards, with Michal seconding the nomination.

"Sounds good to me," agreed Billy. "But what about the rumor that you candidated for the pulpit at Cedar Creek last Sunday? Are you even available for this appointment?"

Ben pulled Serenity close. "That's why we were late to the meeting. I did candidate at Cedar Creek. Serenity and I both agree that our love for one another supersedes any other component of life. She has indicated complete willingness to walk away from involvement here in the Spire because of our love. But I won't be going to Cedar Creek. And it's her fault."

"Not entirely." She poked him in the side. "It seems as if he doesn't meet the Timothy Three qualifications after all."

"One man on the pulpit committee convinced a majority that "husband of one wife" disqualified bachelors from the pastoral office. They voted me down."

"Which means that three other bachelors are free to offer him the position we all know Dr. Edwards planned for him from the beginning," said Daniel.

And Serenity agreed.

# Chapter Twenty-Four

P lanning for the biggest day of their lives began with Sere and Ben's first disagreement as an engaged couple.

"A funeral and wedding on the same day?" Serenity's objection stemmed from the logistics of planning rather than any hesitancy to get married as soon as possible, a distinction she felt made her position unassailable. "Impossible. What in the world are you thinking?"

"If that is more than a rhetorical question, I will tell you what I'm thinking." Ben had decided the day they talked in the Hall of Heroes that far too many years had been wasted to think about any extensive engagement period. They had both had ample time to prepare. "What I'm thinking has found its best expression in the words of Jim Elliot, 'Live to the hilt every situation you believe to be the will of God.'"

Her acceptance of that quote set in motion a whirlwind of activity on the part of all those involved in the Spire, until Verna proclaimed it to be as intensive as any of the manifold Freedom Projects she helped Dr. Edwards organize through the years.

The early morning interment at Chapel Hill Memorial Gardens definitely qualified as the most understated of the day's events. Tyler and Ricci, Tony and Beth, Michal and Amelia, Billy and Verna joined Serenity and Ben as workers lowered the unusual double casket into the ground. A skeptical funeral director had reluctantly agreed to their desire not to separate Ernst and Leila in their graves. The layout artist and etcher at Hinderuth Monument Company proved far more cooperative. A small replica of the Spire inscribed with the words "Together Forever" united two marble headstones with names and dates. At the bottom center of the memorial a grinning Humpty Dumpty sat on a wall looking down on the smiling face of Cinderella.

Ben spoke quietly, describing the scene as the couple they all loved entered heaven.

"At one end of a promenade of gold, a crowd spills out onto a sea of glass, like a huge mirror, but transformed into a multitude of colors by what appear to be flames or fireworks continually exploding under its surface. Rising from the glass sea, row upon row of bleachers appear, packed with members of a magnificent chorale. An orchestra of a thousand harps accompanies them as they sing an oratorio greater than anything ever written by Mozart or Handel. 'Great and marvelous are thy works, Lord God Almighty: just and true are thy ways, thou King of saints.' Voices cascade through the air and echo off the golden gates surrounding the city. An inner voice directs them to seats which they realize must be one of at least five hundred million in the vast arena, and yet every place in the entire stadium seems like a front row, just as in the Spire. The same inner voice seems to whisper, 'If you had been the only person on earth, I still would have died for you. You have been chosen, a special person. Enter into the joy of the Lord.'"

"And then they see Him. Seated on a throne. High and lifted up above the very center of the stadium. They understand why every seat feels like a front seat. The two of them sit alone, even though surrounded by thousands upon thousands of men and angels. They have his undivided attention, and with an overwhelming sense of awe they give him theirs as well.

The Lamb of God who takes away the sin of the world.

The King of kings and Lord of lords.

The Great I Am.

Creator of the universe.

The Son of God.

Jesus, name above all names!"

"Awestruck. Speechless. Humbled. Amazed. The entire crowd stands to their feet only to drop to their knees. Dr. Edwards opens his mouth to give thanks, only to close it again when the man who never lacked for words can discover no adequate words at all. Leila bows her head, only to find that she cannot resist looking deep into those eyes of love. Eyes which have watched over her through all her years of mental turmoil. Together they worship—not with hands or knees or tongue. Those ritual forms so familiar to us on earth seem totally inadequate in heaven. Worship comes from the heart, the soul, the mind, the strength."

"It's their first day in heaven, and without ever exploring its outer reaches, without ever seeing the mansion he's been preparing, without ever riding on a cloud or talking to saints like Abraham and David and Esther, without yet partaking in any of the marvelous heavenly adventures that await as the ages roll on—they are satisfied. It's their first day in heaven, and they have already discovered who heaven is all about."

The funeral service broadcast from the Spire began at noon. No entourage drove slowly through the streets of Kansas City. No casket sat in state. No mourners filed solemnly past earthly remains speaking in pious whispers. Instead, an estimated one hundred million viewers worldwide thrilled to the testimonies of those whose lives had been transformed by the preaching ministry of Dr. Ernst Edwards.

Tyler Ravenal recalled the jubilant rejoicing shared with Ernst the day they realized sales of the Reversal of Babel app exceeded one million.

Michal DeLoran confessed to the world that he was not the Prophet, describing the plans he had formulated with Edwards for the development of indigenous hymnody for each of the people groups enjoying the biblical expositions from InSpire Ministries.

The renowned sculptor of an award winning re-creation of the Transfiguration in a garden in Stockholm, Sweden, shared the story of how he had been awakened in the middle of the night by a call from Kansas City, surprised by a voice offering to underwrite his vision, which up to that time had only appeared in miniature.

Billy Wilson spoke for exactly five minutes, crediting the optimism of Dr. Edwards as the spur which prompted him to walk away from a multimillion-dollar football contract in order to kickoff Wilson Sports Rallies.

The most recent recipient of the Nobel Prize in Literature, Ricci Morris, recounted her early efforts, unsuccessfully submitting her first novel to more than forty-seven publishers before agreeing to a contract with InSpire Ministries, a firm which had never before produced any books except Edwards's sermons.

Daniel Ellicott zoomed in from Kandahar, greeting his fellow countrymen in Pashto and Dari, before reverting back to English as he announced the establishment of the Ernst Edwards Free University, dedicated to providing tuition-free education worldwide to all those who desired to pursue theological training.

He introduced Mostafa who shared his testimony of faith in God as a result of the ministry of the Spire and the Reversal of Babel app. He was succeeded by women and men from Iraq, Nepal, Guam, Ireland, Nigeria, North Korea, Peru, Bangladesh, Moldovia, and sixteen other countries watching the funeral on Zoom who also testified of the grace of God that had brought salvation to their lives. Each spoke in their native tongue, and all those listening worldwide heard them in their own language.

Tyler returned to the platform to invite everyone to listen to the original gospel message included with the purchase of every translation app sold around the world. "He being dead yet speaketh," was the verse from Hebrews which he shared as he introduced Dr. Edwards's familiar voice presenting the truth of God's word at his own funeral.

Finally, Serenity introduced Dr. Edwards's successor.

"He has always been somewhat of a weirdo," she joked, pointing out the man who sat on the platform behind her in the doctoral regalia of his alma mater, something she had convinced him to wear for the service. "With his mother Ricci constantly in the books pursuing her bachelor's degree, he decided to further his own education and taught himself to read at age three. French cartoons became his nanny, and a proclivity toward languages soon added Spanish and German to his mental lexicon. One day while watching InSpire services, he heard Dr. Edwards mention Greek. He mastered that before he was ten. He started reading through the Bible several times a year, translating passages from Greek, and later Hebrew, while still a teen. Completing his homeschool curriculum at age fourteen elicited early enrollment to the online program at Indiana University. His first college degree was granted when he was seventeen, and his first doctorate awarded at age twenty. Six years ago my father became his mentor. Six days ago I became his fiancé. With the unanimous approval of the executive board of InSpire Ministries, I take great pride in introducing my father's chosen successor, and my soon to be husband, Dr. Benjamin Morris."

The double wedding took place at Bride of the Lamb Wedding Venue in front of a group of invited guests and hundreds of park visitors who simply loved to attend weddings. The fact that the venue hosted weddings daily made it possible for Ricci and Serenity to pull together flowers, decorations, programs, and a reception in under a week, plans that normally would have extended over months and months. Dresses had to come from off the rack, but Kansas City boasted numerous bridal shops which were thrilled to participate in those preparations.

Deke and Phil served as ushers, relishing the prospect of asking guests if they wanted to sit on the bride's side or groom's side, even though most of them had no idea whose wedding they were attending. The stunned looks on faces when handed a program revealed the depth of that surprise. Viewed from one direction the program cover read:

> "Tyler Ravenel and Ricci Morris welcome you to the wedding of their son Benjamin Morris and Serenity Edwards, daughter of Ernst and Leila Edwards."

Looked at from the other side the program read:

> "Benjamin Morris welcomes you to the wedding of his mother Ricci Morris and his father Tyler Ravenel."

If that wasn't confusing enough, Serenity Edwards was listed as the bridesmaid for Ricci and Benjamin as the best man for Tyler. The program also indicated that Dr. Benjamin Morris would be officiating the Ravenel wedding, while Tyler would be standing up for him during the Morris ceremony with Ricci as Serenity's matron of honor.

Tyler and Ben took their places at the front of the chapel as first Ricci and then Serenity entered from the back. Ricci Morris wore a cocktail length, A-line gown in light ivory. Vintage flowers in whitework adorned the bodice and cascaded down to kiss the hem. Serenity floated down the aisle in a floor-length sleeveless ball-gown, trailed by a six-foot train of Chantilly lace. Both women carried bridal bouquets of white roses, with one red rose in each arrangement in memory of Leila Edwards.

At the front of the room, the two men escorted their brides onto the platform. Leaving Serenity's side for the time being, Ben took his place in front of his mother and father.

"Who giveth this woman to be married to this man?" he asked, and then answered his own question immediately. "I do."

The Ravenels had chosen the traditional wedding vows for their ceremony, and Ben led them through the familiar words, occasionally blinking back tears of joy and drawing strength from Serenity's presence.

"I, Ricci Morris, take thee, Tyler Ravenel, to be my wedded husband, to have and to hold from this day forward, for better, for worse, for richer, for poorer, in sickness and in health, to love and to cherish, till death us do part, according to God's holy ordinance; and thereto I pledge thee my troth."

Once Ben had introduced his parents to the assembly as Mr. and Mrs. Tyler Ravenel, the newlyweds took their place as best man and matron of honor next to him and Serenity. Michal DeLoran walked onto the platform with an acoustic guitar and sang a poignant song about eternal life and eternal love. He had written it specifically for this day in which both farewells and felicitations would play such prominent roles.

After the song, Billy Wilson came forward to face the wedding party, resplendent in a tuxedo which had been altered to fit his rugged frame.

"May I have five minutes of your valuable time?" he began, and the crowd which had been moved to tears by Michal's performance broke out into applause.

Serenity and Ben had written their own vows. Following Billy's short message, they turned to face one another and joined hands while Ricci held both bouquets.

Serenity began.

"Ben. Life with you will be a never-ending adventure. I choose to walk that path into the future by your side, not leading as I often desire to do, nor following as you sometimes expect, but hand in hand. I promise to tolerate you during those times when your dogmatic pronouncements tend to make you intolerable. I promise to honor you when your naïve foolishness encourages me rather to laugh. I promise to cherish you even on those days when you become so heavenly minded you are of no earthly good. My love will belong to you, and you alone, as long as the stars shine down and little green apples grow."

Without waiting for "you may now kiss the bride" permission from Billy, Ben embraced her and lingered his lips on hers until Deke and Phil began to blow the referee's whistles they had brought for just such a possibility. Only then did he share his own vows.

"Serenity. I feel as if we are poised at the apex of the Fall of Man Roller Coaster, the one your father called Serenity's Tornado. Our journey up to this point has been slow. What follows today may take our breath away. Unanticipated twists and turns, jolts and bumps, incredible thrills, and hair-raising experiences of living with you have become my magnificent obsession. When Christ loved the church, He gave himself to make her radiant. I promise to give myself in like manner to you. I will honor and bestow careful consideration on your disputations, even when they lack logical perspicacity. I will cherish you at those hopefully rare moments when your tenacity rises to the level of obstinacy. My love belongs to you, and you alone, even if the stars fall from the sky and those little green apples end up as sour applesauce."

Billy grabbed their hands and raised them high, as if they had both gone twelve rounds in the World Wrestling Association. "Ladies and Gentlemen, I give you the winners—Dr. and Mrs. Benjamin Morris." Returning their hands to the grasp of each other, he continued. "And NOW, you may kiss your bride."

This time they paid no attention at all to the whistles.